# THE LILAC CODE

The Sisters, Texas Mystery Series
Book Seven

## BECKI WILLIS

ISBN: 1-947686-05-4
ISBN-13: 978-1-947686-05-2

# CONTENTS

# ACKNOWLEDGMENTS

Editing by SJS Editorial Services
Cover Design by dienel96.

Photography of *The Columbia Inn at Peralynna* is the author's personal photograph and used with permission by the Lynns.

Special Note: The character of Logan McKee is 'on loan' from Dr. Cynthia Lynn, who retains full rights to her creation. She generously allowed me to introduce her character prior to releasing her own series, debuting next year. In return, I am gifting the character of Sophie to her, to use as she pleases.

# PROLOGUE

CIA Headquarters, Langely, Virginia

Only a handful were present. A half-dozen high-level officials and agents, gathered round the conference table behind closed doors.

"Again, I don't have to tell you how important this mission is." The director of the CIA addressed the solemn group, his expression heavy. "It is imperative that we retrieve the case and crack The Lilac Code."

"Do we have an eye on Kalypso?" There was an edge in the general's voice, but the four stars on his shoulder gave him that right.

"You know as well as I do, General," the DCI admitted, "no one ever quite 'has their eye' on Kalypso. The woman is a master of disguises, just as her name, *'she who conceals*,' suggests. However, sources report her last known location as Nicaragua."

"I don't like it," the general blustered. "We know the case is coming in through the Houston ship channel. I don't care if it is two thousand miles from Managua, that's too close for comfort."

"We have our best officers on it, General, sir." The CIA's deputy director broke in. "We have both Kalypso and Murdoch under heavy surveillance. Our sources assure us that Kalypso has made no effort to leave her home in Managua. As for Murdoch, the moment he arrives back on US soil, we will work in tandem with the FBI to obtain the case. I can assure you, sir, we won't take our eyes off him, or from the case."

Another man spoke up. "How do we know Murdoch can be trusted to deliver the case? The man is little more than a mercenary. He shows no loyalty to either side."

The DCI's grim smile lacked humor. "Murdoch is loyal to the almighty dollar. Have no doubt, Lieutenant General, we're prepared to pay top dollar for that case."

"He's right, General, sir. Lieutenant General." The CIA officer in charge of the mission spoke for the first time. The woman dipped her blond head with a respectful nod to each man, before turning to address the other man at the table. "Mr. Vice President, I will personally oversee the exchange. We're throwing an elaborate cocktail party tomorrow evening, so that joint special operatives, key agents, and high-level security officers can be nearby, should Kalypso make a surprise appearance."

"I trust this party and the exchange will take place at a secure location?"

"Absolutely, sir. We've used the house on numerous occasions, as it allows for excellent surveillance. We already have security teams in place and fully prepared. We have every reason to expect a smooth transaction, sir." The operations officer spoke with confidence.

"Excellent."

"That still leaves the message, itself," the general worried. He clearly did not share the same confidence as the case officer. "Without the message, the case does us no good."

The negative remark didn't sit well with the officer.

The DCI shot her a silent warning before turning to the general with his best and most reassuring smile. "I understand your worry, General. You have every right to doubt the integrity of Murdoch and Kalypso. Neither can be trusted. But one thing you cannot doubt is the dedication and capability of our officers. We have our top people handling this matter. Trust me, sir."

He looked each man squarely in the eye as he reiterated his promise.

"We will retrieve the message. We will keep the case from falling into Kalypso's hands. And we will crack the Lilac Code."

# 1

"I have a bad feeling about this trip."

Madison Reynolds glanced at her friend in concern. "You okay?" she asked. "I know we were late leaving, but we'll make our plane with plenty of time. There's no need to be nervous."

"It's not that," Genesis Baker said, blond hair dancing as she shook her head in denial. "It's this whole trip," she murmured, staring out the passenger's side window. "I have a feeling something bad is going to happen."

For once, their roles were reversed. Normally, Madison was the worrier and Genny was the cheerleader. "You're just worried, leaving so close to the wedding," she reassured her friend. "Everything will be fine. We'll have a great girl trip and be home in plenty of time to handle those pesky last-minute details."

"You're just missing that handsome fiancé of yours," their backseat companion piped in. "If I had a man as fine as Cutter Montgomery, I'd hate to leave, too."

"Uh, you kind of do," Madison reminded her grandmother. "Cutter is the spitting image of his grandfather." She glanced at the older woman through the rearview mirror and noticed how she squirmed. "Don't tell me you two are arguing again."

"The stubborn old goat wants to get married," Granny Bert huffed. "I keep telling him that boat sailed sixty-odd years ago. I have no intentions of marrying him, then or now."

"I don't know, Granny," Genny teased. Her frown melted away and reemerged as a smile. "We could have a double wedding. Grandfather and grandson. Might be sort of cool."

"Until one of his ex-wives showed up and stirred a ruckus," the older woman sniffed. It still bothered her that the man who claimed to love only her had married a half-dozen other women. "No," she insisted, "February fourteenth is your day, girl. And this doubles as your bachelorette trip, so sit back and enjoy it."

The frown returned. "I'll try. But I just have this nagging feeling that something bad is fixin' to happen."

"Your uptight friend behind the wheel made me promise not to hire any male strippers," Granny Bert complained. "With you judging that cooking contest, it doesn't leave much time to get into trouble. So relax. What could possibly go wrong?"


Forty minutes later, they had their first answer. A sea of taillights swam before them. In the distance, emergency vehicles worked a major wreck.

"We're never going to make it on time," Genny wailed. Each glance at the clock told a more dismal tale.

"Maddy, can't you weave your way through this traffic? Turn your emergency flashers on. Someone is bound to let you through."

BECKI WILLIS

"I can't do that, Granny Bert," Madison chided.

"If we get stopped, I'll say I'm having a heart attack. At my age, they'd be hard-pressed to doubt me." The eighty-one-year-old glared at the stand-still traffic clogging all four lanes of the interstate. "We sit here much longer," she snorted, "and I may not have to fake a thing. I knew there was a reason I avoided coming to Houston."

"I thought it was because of that incident you had at the Astrodome," Genny said, innocently enough.

"Genesis Baker, how dare you bring that up, after all these years? If I've told you once, I've told you girls a thousand times. It was all just a misunderstanding."

"That's not how the news reported it," Madison reminded her grandmother.

Granny Bert gave another loud snort. "Fake news," she insisted.

While her grandmother pouted from the backseat, traffic resumed at the pace of an injured snail.

"If you can get off up here," Genny advised, studying the navigation app on her phone, "I think we could take a side street and wind our way over to the airport."

"The question is, will it be any faster?"

Genny motioned to the sea of red. "It's gotta be better than this, don't you think?"

Madison debated the issue until the last moment, but in the time it took to inch toward the exit, another six minutes had evaporated. Madison put on her blinker, nosed the car to the right, and left the gridlocked freeway. "You'll have to guide me, Genny. I'm not familiar with this part of town."

Granny Bert harrumphed as she eyed the colorful graffiti decorating the street signs. "I'd be worried if you were. They don't feature this neighborhood in *Better Homes and Gardens* for a reason."

"Too late now," Madison muttered. She double-checked that all doors and windows were securely locked. "Let's hope we'll be through it soon."

"Stay on this street for three...no, four lights," Genny directed. "Then make a left. We should be out of the worst of it by then. I recognize a high school in that area."

"Hang around here too long, and we'll get more of an education than any of us bargained for," Granny Bert predicted. "I'm pretty sure I just saw a drug deal going down, and that hooker back there didn't have enough clothes on to cover the goods she's peddling. Let's just say if she gave a striptease, it would be a mighty short act."

"Granny, whatever you do, don't make eye contact. Don't provoke anyone." Madison nibbled on her bottom lip. "On second thought, maybe you should just sit back and close your eyes until we get to the airport."

"Are you kidding me? Who needs a male stripper, when we have this fine and educational neighborhood? It's just getting interesting." The older woman sat up in the seat so she could better see.

Madison drove as fast as she dared through the downtown streets. She dutifully counted off four lights, breathing a sigh of relief as she made the left-hand turn onto a larger thoroughfare.

"How far are we from the airport now?" she asked her friend.

Avoiding a direct response, Genny went with a brisk, "Don't ask, just drive."

"That far, huh?"

"I told you I should drive," Granny Bert chirped. "I could've had us there by now."

"Arriving in body bags doesn't count," Madison replied sweetly. "And we haven't missed that plane yet. Have faith.”

Genny was still unusually glum. “We're going to need it,” she murmured. “Because I'm telling you, something bad is going to happen on this trip.”


“I'm beginning to see your point,” Madison told her friend as they rushed through the airport. “If nothing else, this trip is getting off to a memorable start.” She readjusted the bag swinging from her shoulder and navigated both rolling bags around a slow-moving pedestrian. Luggage free, her grandmother led their charge to the gate with a fast pace. Madison had difficulty keeping up.

Out of breath from all but running the last bit of the way, Genny only nodded. “I see the gate,” she panted, nodding forward.

“What are you two complaining about?” Granny Bert asked, not bothering to slow down as she flung the words over her shoulder. “I got us through that security line, lickety split. Without my brilliant act back there, we'd still be standing in line.”

Her grandmother had a point. After seeing the outrageous line snaking backward from the security checkpoint, Granny Bert grabbed a wheelchair, plopped down into it, and began fanning herself. A few moans and whimpers later, the three of them were whisked to the front of the line, given priority passage through screening, and even garnered a ride with airport-courtesy transport. The driver offered to request another chair for Granny at the end of the line, but she declined. Slipping him a wink and a folded bill, she convinced him to call the gate and insist they hold the plane for them. She then jumped off the cart and led their small entourage the remainder of the way.

Luckily for them, the gate was just around the corner.

A fuzzy voice rattled from the public announcement system. "Would Madison Reynolds, Genesis Baker, and Bertha Cessna report immediately to Gate 8B. 8B."

Madison was mortified. "I can't believe they're calling our names on the airport speaker!"

"I can't believe we made it!" Genny panted.

Granny Bert greeted the attendant with a broad smile and motioned upward. "That's us. They're holding the door for us."

"I'm afraid it's a full flight and you'll have to take whatever seat is available," the attendant said. She eyed their carry-on luggage with a frown. "You may have to check your luggage. I'm sure the overhead bins are full by now."

"It's only three pieces," Madison assured her. "These bags are our personal items."

That earned her a prim, "There's a limit to one per passenger, and they all must fit securely under the seat."

"They do," Madison said with a confidence she didn't feel. "And this one's hers."

"Has all my medicine in it," Granny Bert added, allowing her shoulders to sag. Her voice didn't sound nearly as strong as it had moments before. She patted her chest, struggling to pull in a deep breath. "I hope I don't have to go all the way to the back of the plane. I'm all tuckered out. Who would think an airport would run out of wheelchairs?"

"Are you all right, ma'am?" the attendant asked. She was suddenly full of concern, particularly at the implication that the airport had failed one of its passengers.

The wizened old woman managed a weak nod. "I

will be, as soon as I get on that plane. There's an operation waiting for me in Baltimore."

"I'll request a front seat," the woman said, reaching for her two-way radio.

"Bless your heart, child." Granny Bert offered a weak smile as she shuffled ahead. "Give me your hand, Maddy, and help your old granny to the plane."

When they were out of earshot, Madison hissed, "Granny, you have to stop pulling this con! There's no operation waiting for you, and you know it!"

"Sure there is," she grinned. "Operation Par-tay."

"Granny!"

"Can I help it if she drew the wrong conclusions? I never once mentioned a surgical procedure."

Madison blew out an exasperated sigh and muttered beneath her breath. "What am I going to do with you?"

They stepped onto the crowded plane, where two attendants waited to assist Granny Bert. A vacant seat had mysteriously appeared in the second row, thanks to a generous passenger.

"I'm sorry, you ladies won't be able to sit with her," one of the attendants said. "I believe there's one seat at the rear of the plane and another on row 35."

"Leave the bag with my medicine," Granny Bert requested weakly. Having planned to sit together on the open-seating flight, their snacks were compiled into one bag. The old woman's grip was amazingly strong as she snagged it from Maddy's hand.

"You ladies take a seat. I'll find a place for your luggage," the male attendant offered.

Madison relinquished their bags and squeezed past him, headed for the back. She avoided direct eye contact with the other passengers, afraid she would see contempt in their faces. Their late arrival threw the flight off its tight schedule, and until they were seated, and their luggage stowed, the plane was still grounded.

Halfway down the aisle, she heard a whispered rustle and dared a glance to her left. The animated trio smiled at her and waved. No doubt, they recognized her from the reality television series *Home Again*. HOME TV faithfully reran episodes of the popular makeover show, hoping to entice Madison into doing another season, but she steadfastly refused. Having her personal life broadcast on national television had been a necessary evil, but with the remodel complete, she insisted her televisions days were behind her.

Madison smiled at the mini fan club and moved along, encouraged to see that not everyone on the flight was hostile.

She made the mistake of eye contact with a man behind them. His stoic face was a study in impatience. Icy gray eyes bore into hers, conveying his extreme displeasure. He had the look of a man always in motion, wound tight to react fast. Despite the strap at his waist, he seemed perched on the edge of his seat, ready for action.

*Oops*, Madison thought, averting her eyes. *Guess we made him late.*

At least the woman two rows behind him looked more amiable. Her face was best described as impassive, but it was a welcomed change from the beady-eyed man's open hostility.

Leaving the first available spot for her friend, Madison trudged to the rear of the plane. She squeezed into the middle seat, squashed between two very overweight passengers. The good news, she decided, was that if the plane experienced turbulence, she had plenty of cushion.

Buckling in, she hoped for a quiet flight and a

much-needed nap. Some sort of ruckus mid-plane left a child crying and flight attendants scurrying, but she still hoped for a nap. They had left The Sisters before dawn to reach Houston and catch their morning flight. After the stress of driving in stop-and-go traffic, a detour through the 'hood, and their mad rush through the airport, her nerves were frayed around the edges.

Whether she wanted to admit it or not, Genny's premonition of trouble nibbled on the back of her mind. Maddy wasn't exactly superstitious, but if her usually upbeat and cheerful friend was this worried about the trip, she could hardly ignore the potential for problems ahead.

Her hopes of peace evaporated when her companion on the left introduced herself. Angie from Annapolis chattered from the moment they taxied down the runway until the attendant took their orders for complimentary refreshments. After ordering a caffeine-laced soda—*as if she needs any more energy*, Madison cringed—the chatterbox finally paused long enough to ask, "And what takes you to Baltimore?"

"My friend is a chef, and she's judging a celebrity bake-off. Since she's getting married in two weeks, this trip doubles as a bachelorette trip."

"Girl trip!" Angie said in a sing-song voice, attempting to wiggle in the tightly packed space. Madison absorbed the blows with barely a grimace. "And how delightful!" She clasped her hands together in glee. "I love those kinds of things, especially when they offer samples to the audience! Are they selling tickets to the event? Where is it being held?"

"I think it's about a half hour from Baltimore, at some designer kitchen showroom. They often film television cooking shows there, from what I understand."

Angie from Annapolis nodded vigorously. "I know exactly where you mean! I love to go there and see all the newest appliances. In my mind, heaven must look exactly like *Fretz Kitchens*."

"Oh, so you're a cook?" Madison asked, more from politeness than curiosity.

"Oh, no. Just a fan of fine food. When did you say the competition is? I'd love to get my hands on those tickets!"

"I'm not sure if they're selling tickets, but the first bake-off starts tomorrow morning."

"Did you upgrade to Wi-Fi for this flight?" Eager Angie asked. "We could look up tickets."

"No, I didn't. I had hoped to nap." Madison added the last as a subtle hint.

Too subtle, apparently, for Angie to notice.

"I never sleep on planes. If we're going to crash, I want to know about it from the first sputter of the engine, so I can start saying my prayers."

Hoping the woman's words about crashing didn't carry throughout the cabin and cause panic, Madison quickly changed the subject. "If you know the area, what can you tell me about our hotel? We're staying at the *Presidential Hotel* in Columbia."

Angie's eyebrows shot upward. "What can I tell you? I can tell you that you *won't* be staying there!"

Her strange response drew a frown from Madison. "I don't understand. It has a five-star rating and is apparently close to the contest venue. What's wrong with the hotel?"

"Oh, it's a wonderful hotel. At least, it *was*. Haven't you heard? There was a huge fire there this morning and gutted the entire building."

Madison gasped. "Seriously? We had no idea!"

"It's been all over the news. In fact, I saw the story playing on the airport news monitors. Didn't you see it? Apparently, they haven't ruled out arson."

"We were running late," Madison murmured, her tone distracted. Her mind raced ahead. Was this the trouble Genny had foreseen? "I wonder where we'll stay now."

"I know just the place!" Angie answered, clasping her hands together again. *"The Columbia Inn at Peralynna!"*

Not realizing she spoke her worry aloud, Madison hadn't expected an answer. She looked at her companion in surprise.

"Yes," Angie beamed, nodding vigorously. "You simply *have* to stay there. It's a wonderful house, and it's full of mystique and over-the-top elegance. It was originally a private home, built to mimic a CIA safe house."

"Why would someone want to build a CIA safe house as their home?"

"It's a fascinating story. When you get internet service, you can read all about it. The owner's parents were both agents and she grew up abroad, in a safe house that looked more like a grand mansion. You should see this place. Balconies, turrets, and all kinds of secret nooks. Rumor has it there's even three hidden staircases in the house."

"Sounds like the Big House," Madison mused.

"You've never seen a prison like this!" Angie assured her.

Madison didn't bother to correct her. The Big House was the moniker people had given to Juliet Blakely's stately old mansion back home, the very mansion that Madison and her twins now lived in, thanks to Granny Bert's generosity, a healthy dose of her conniving ways, and the good people at HOME TV.

Her companion continued extolling the virtues of

the home turned boutique hotel. Madison managed a few questions but had little opportunity to do anything other than listen.

"There's seventeen or eighteen suites, and all of them are unique. I've only stayed there once, but I attended a luncheon there with a group from the historical society, and they gave us a mini tour. The history of the place is fascinating. Seriously, you must check it out. The moment we get off this plane, you need to call and book a room. There's not a lot of tourists in our area this time of year, so they should have a vacancy."

"I'll do that," Madison promised. In truth, the place did sound interesting.

And if Angie from Annapolis was right, it sounded as if their reservations at the *Presidential Hotel* had just been canceled.

# 2

Seated on the next-to-last row of the plane, Madison was among the last passengers to exit. She stopped long enough to collect her carry-on from the overhead bin where the attendant had stashed it, promised Angie from Annapolis she would look up the hotel, and hurried to find Genny and Granny Bert.

They waited for her on a bench in the concourse. Granny Bert people-watched as Genny bit her lip and studied her phone. Even from a distance, Madison could see the worry on her friend's face.

"Nothing like bringing up the rear," she said by way of greeting them.

Genny's blond head snapped up. "I knew this trip was jinxed!" she wailed. "You'll never believe what happened!"

"I heard. Our hotel burned down."

Genny's eyes widened. "How did you already hear? I just got the email. Was it on your news feed?"

"Who needs news feeds when you're sitting next to Angie from Annapolis? The woman is a walking information source. Seriously, I think Reuters gets their information from *her*."

"What now? I don't know much about the Columbia area. I know some good hotels in DC, but the traffic is a nightmare."

"Don't worry," Madison assured her, "Angie had information about that, too. She says there's a place we simply *must* stay. *The Columbia Inn at Peralynna,* right there in Columbia."

"I'll look it up," Genny said, already entering it into her phone's search engine. "I hope they have an opening at this late date."

"If not, I was sitting next to a lovely gentleman who offered us his yacht for the week," Granny Bert said. "I have his business card here somewhere."

"Ooh, this place looks nice!" Genny said with enthusiasm as she perused the hotel's website. "Look at this."

Madison peered at the screen. "Even nicer than the first hotel," she agreed.

"At this point, anything would be nicer than the *Burning Beds,*" smirked Granny Bert.

While Genny continued on her phone, Madison looked around the airport for signage. "Which way to ground transportation, I wonder? Oh, over there." She put a hand to her rumbling tummy. "As soon as we get our car, we need to find a place to eat. *Someone* I know"—she threw her grandmother a pointed look—"hogged the snack bag all to herself."

"Hey, I shared with Gilbert."

"Who's Gilbert?"

"My friend with the yacht. Weren't you listening?"

Madison wiggled her ear with her finger. "All I've done for the past three hours is listen. Angie stopped talking only long enough to guzzle down two Cokes, both our peanuts, and to beg me for tickets to the celebrity cook-off."

Genny held up her phone. "Is this hotel okay with y'all? It looks pretty cool."

"I can sleep anywhere," Granny Bert claimed.

"Give me a pillow and a blanket, and I'm good."

"These pillows and blankets come with Tempurpedic mattresses and a five-star rating," Genny informed her.

"And mystery," Madison added, wagging her brows. "There's supposedly a secret staircase or two, and a tie to espionage." She said the last in a hushed whisper and a dramatic gesture.

"I always thought I'd make a good spy," Granny Bert mused. "'Course, raising four rowdy boys, your father in particular, and holding public office for so many years, I guess I was a spy, of sorts. Just without the element of danger."

"This trip is my vacation," Madison proclaimed, establishing ground rules right from the beginning. "No danger, no dead bodies, no excitement. Just a few days of fun and relaxation."

Granny Bert frowned at her granddaughter. "Where's the fun in that? Sounds rather boring to me."

"Exactly. Boring is good. Boring is relaxing."

Her grandmother disagreed. "This might be why you and I don't vacation together more often. We have vastly different views on what constitutes 'fun.'"

"It looks like they have a couple of rooms available," Genny said, still engrossed with her phone. "I can walk and talk at the same time. You lead, I'll follow."

After shooting off a brief text about landing safely, Madison gathered their luggage. She gave her grandmother an exasperated look as she slung the considerably lighter snack bag onto her shoulder. As she pulled their rolling bags behind her, she complained, "Either this suitcase got heavier or I've gotten weaker."

"Give me that handle. I can roll my own bag."

Granny Bert took over without losing a beat. "And eat a granola bar so you won't be so grouchy."

They made their way across the airport, following signs toward ground transportation and the rental car shuttle. While they waited for Granny Bert to visit the little girl's room for the second time, Maddy read a text from Brash.

To simplify matters, her fiancé was staying at the Big House with the twins while she was gone. It also served as a trial run for when they got married. His teenage daughter Megan was there, too, already claiming one of the third-floor turret rooms as her own. Madison smiled at his message, sent a quick reply with a heart emoji, and tucked her phone away. She could hardly wait for her own wedding, set a month after Genny and Cutter's.

A little girl with dark braids approached Maddy with a shy smile. "Here, pretty lady," she said, extending her hand.

Madison was hesitant to accept anything in an airport, even from a child, until she saw the simple drawing. A lop-sided flower graced a small square of paper, along with a few crudely printed letters. The scrambled letters—some drawn backwards, some in lower case, others in capitals—made no sense. Madison recalled countless such notes from Bethani and Blake when they were the same age as the little girl. They loved practicing their letters, long before they could spell or write their names.

"Why, thank you," Madison said with a smile. "This is for me?"

The little girl nodded shyly.

"It's lovely," Madison assured her. "Thank you."

The girl turned apologetically to Genny. "I don't have one for you."

"That's okay, honey. I bet my friend will share hers

with me. Will that be okay?"

The little girl nodded so vigorously it sent her braids bouncing. Without another word, she skipped her way into the restroom, almost colliding with Granny Bert.

Madison stuffed the note into her pocket and hurried forward to offer her grandmother a steadying hand. Despite brushing away the help, it took the older woman a moment to regain her balance.

"What's the matter with folks these days, sending their young 'uns into a bathroom, unattended?" she grumbled. "Don't they know there's perverts in the world?"

"Maybe she's traveling with her father," Genny suggested. "That guy over there with the dark glasses seems to be with her."

"Then they should use the family restrooms or the 'I can't decide' restrooms so he can go in with her."

Before her grandmother could go off onto a tangent about the status of public restrooms, Madison urged her forward. "Let's find that shuttle and get our car," she suggested.

"Now that we've changed hotels," Genny pitched in, her tone much perkier than it was this morning, "I can't wait to check into our room!"

"See? All that worry for nothing. We got off to a rocky start and our original reservations may have fallen through, but all's well that ends well. Nothing bad is going to happen."

"She's right," Granny Bert agreed. "Despite my granddaughter's idea of fun, this will be a girl trip we'll never forget."

# 3

As normal for February, the Texas weather turned with the whim of a typical Southern belle. A front blew down from the Artic, transforming the morning's sunny sixty-one into a blustery thirty-nine by noon. The darkening clouds gathered like a pouting debutante, promising a cold end to the day.

"Not a problem for us," Cutter Montgomery said with an easy grin. "We'll be indoors the whole afternoon."

Blake, Madison's sixteen-year-old son, staggered through the door behind him, carrying the opposite end of a bulky leather loveseat.

"Remind me again," the teen muttered. "Why did we agree to this?"

"Because you love Genny and you want to help surprise her." With a charming smile that was completely lost upon his male companion, Cutter added, "That, and because I promised to reward you with pizza."

"Plus, you took us out of school early," Bethani chimed in. The fireman's smile wasn't lost upon Blake's twin, who knew he only had eyes for his fiancé. Which was fine with her, since she, too, adored her Aunt Genny. It didn't matter that there was no shared blood between them. Genesis Baker was family.

Taking her decorating assignment quite seriously, Bethani pointed to a spot near the fireplace. "Let's see what it looks like over here."

"We moved the couch like fifty times," her brother complained. "Unless I get some of that pizza soon, I'll be too weak to lift my finger, much less this couch."

"Good thing you didn't miss your math class, Mr. Einstein," Megan deCordova snickered, pausing from her task of arranging bronzed western sculptures along the rustic mantel. "You obviously can't count. You moved the couch maybe a dozen times, tops. And don't worry. Even though you ate in the school cafeteria an hour ago, Dad will be here with the proper nourishment at any moment."

Ignoring their banter, Bethani tipped her blond head to one side as she stood back and inspected the room as a whole. "Blake, scoot yours back just a little. Just enough that the leg of the loveseat is still on the rug."

Megan's auburn hair bounced across her shoulders as she nodded in agreement. "You have to anchor it, or else you'll have a floating rug," their soon-to-be stepsister explained. "We learned that on *Kiki's Kustomworks*. This is definitely her best season yet, I think."

Blake eyed the spotted brown and white cowhide in question. "So, in this case, you'd have a floating cow." He turned to Cutter, his blue eyes twinkling. "Next thing you know, you'll have the cow jumping over the moon."

"My bride will be over the moon, when she sees this room," the fireman predicted. "In all seriousness, I appreciate the help, y'all. I told Genny the furniture was on back-order, so this will be a huge surprise when she walks in and sees it."

"I know she's going to love it!" Bethani clapped her hands together in delight. "This room looks like a picture in a magazine. And so does the kitchen."

Her gaze wandered through the open arch, trimmed in hand-hewn beams, to the spacious kitchen beyond. The old farmhouse originally belonged to Cutter's grandparents, but he had lovingly restored it to this newer, improved version. He managed to add modern functionality and style, without sacrificing the integrity or charm of the homestead. Long before he and Genny were an item, he remodeled the kitchen with her in mind. It even had her coveted warming drawers and soapstone countertops.

"I think we should call HOME TV, and show them what you've done with the place," Megan said.

"Oh, no." Cutter's protest was adamant. "Absolutely not."

"I agree," Blake snorted. "Been there, done that. Don't you remember the chaos of being on national television? The next time I'm on camera, they'll be filming me on the pitcher's mound, as the league's youngest recruit in history." He flexed his arms in a victory pump.

Satisfied with the throw pillows she had placed on the loveseat, Bethani straightened and patted her brother on the shoulder. "Twin," she advised in jest, "you really do need to work on your self-esteem. You have so little confidence in yourself."

Brash deCordova heard only the last of the statement, as he pushed through the door with two large boxes of hot, aromatic pizza.

"I know you can't be talking to your brother." His deep baritone boomed across the room as he carried his load to the kitchen island. "If there's one thing Blake doesn't have, it's a lack of self-confidence. Your mom is threatening to buy him a cap with a stretchy headband, just to keep up with his expanding head size."

Brash deposited the boxes and rubbed his hands together. "Man, it's getting cold out there."

Focused on food, the teen wasn't bothered by the weather or the playful insults. He tapped the side of his blond head, following the scent of pepperoni and sausage. "Don't want to crowd all these smarts," he claimed. "Gotta give the brain plenty of room to grow. Hey, didn't you bring pizza for everyone? There's only two boxes here."

Brash cast a suspicious eye at his daughter. "I thought you weren't leaving school until *after* lunch."

Behind stylish specks, Megan rolled her eyes. She wore her turquoise frames today, to match her plaid shirt. In honor of the ranch house they decorated, she and Bethani went with western ensembles today, complete with custom-made cowboy boots, signed by Cutter's very own grandfather. "We *didn't*." She emphasized the word. "You know your future stepson is a bottomless pit." She stepped around the boy and snagged a slice of pizza while she had the chance. "Come on, Beth, get some while you can. You, too, Cutter."

"Use napkins," he warned. "I want this to be a good surprise for Genny, not a greasy mess."

"Geesh, you, too?" Blake bemoaned. "Mr. de read us our rights this morning before school. We have to keep the house clean, the trash cans empty, the laundry folded, the homework done." He reached for his second slice of pizza. "He's worse than Mom."

"When was the last time your mother took a vacation?" Brash asked.

Before the teen could answer, Cutter broke in, "And last fall's trip to the coast doesn't count. That wasn't a pleasure trip. That was to help Genny deal with losing her house and almost losing her life."

Blake wore a thoughtful expression. "I don't remember her ever going anywhere without us," he admitted.

"No, wait. She and Daddy went away for their anniversary a couple of times," Bethani corrected. "But that was... before. Like, ages ago."

"So, we all agree your mom really needs this time away," Brash rationalized. "Not only because she's helping Genny celebrate a special time in her life, but because your mother deserves a little rest and relaxation, too. Agreed?"

Bethani bobbed her blond ponytail. "Definitely."

"Agreed." Blake spoke around his third slice of pizza, now disappearing into his mouth.

"So we don't want her worrying about what's happening back here at home. We want her to know we have things under control, right?"

"Right," Bethani agreed.

Blake nodded as he chewed.

"So the least we can do is keep the house clean, the trash cans empty, and the laundry folded, correct?"

"Don't forget the homework," Megan pitched in sweetly. "You never let me forget mine."

"And the homework done," her father added. "We want Maddy to be proud of us, and how well we can handle things in her absence. We want her to know what a good job she's done, grooming you to become responsible adults and grooming *us* to become a family. A family that works together to keep the household running, even when she's not there to remind us. We want to make her proud of us," he reiterated. "Right, guys?"

Bethani swallowed the sudden lump in her throat as she murmured in agreement. Even Blake slowed down on his pizza intake. Megan's eyes turned misty.

Cutter broke the sentimental moment with his trademark rakish grin. "Heck, after that speech, you make me want to come over and do a load of laundry—and I don't even live there!"

Brash laughed it off. "I'm just saying Maddy deserves this trip. Genny, too. This is the least we can do for them. No worries from our end, so they can enjoy a peaceful, stress-free vacation."

# 4

"Would you look at this place!" Granny Bert gave a low whistle of appreciation as they pulled into the walled estate. "It's even bigger than the Big House. Fancier, too."

"Can you imagine *living* here?" Madison said. "Annette likes to think her Ivy Hall is impressive. I should send her pictures."

"Now that you're on speaking terms again, don't rock the boat," Genny advised. "Remember, your former mother-in-law is taking the kids skiing during your honeymoon."

"Oh, that's right. I definitely don't want to alienate her now." Just thinking of being alone with Brash for the first time made her skin tingle. It was a long six weeks yet to come.

"How cute. You're actually blushing," Genny teased.

Madison made a shooing motion with her fingers. "Don't worry about me. You have your own honeymoon coming up."

"Don't I know it!" Genny said dreamily. Hearts were breaking all around The Sisters, knowing Cutter Montgomery was off the market, but the truth was, he had fallen in love with Genny the moment she first came back to town. It had taken over a year for her to admit her attraction to a man eight years her junior, and to give their relationship a chance.

"Knock off the mushy stuff and take a look at those cars in the parking lot," Granny Bert instructed. "That's a mint-condition '66 Mustang Convertible, just like the one your father used to drive."

"They must have kept that baby in a garage for the past five decades," Genny agreed. "It looks brand new."

"Blake was telling me about a place down in Florida that recreates exact replicas of classic cars. Dear son that he is," Madison's voice dripped with sarcasm, "he thought I might want to know, in case I wanted to give him a copy of a '57 Chevy truck for Christmas."

"Sure, if you have an extra million or so lying around!"

In the understatement of the year, Madison shook her head. "Not this Christmas, I'm afraid."

Her grandmother had already crawled from the backseat. "Let's see what the inside of this snazzy joint looks like."

Madison offered her hand, but the older woman shook it away as she took the steps up the front porch. Genny opened glass-paned double doors leading into the opulent foyer.

With a crystal chandelier above them and Italian tile beneath their feet, Genny's dimpled smile deepened. "I love it already!" she whispered.

"Wow, look at that fireplace in there," Madison murmured, gazing beyond the staircase with its impressive landing. Steps spilled from either side, flanking a curved, cushioned bench against the railings. The fireplace itself stretched as high as the eye could see.

"Welcome to *The Columbia Inn at Peralynna!*" A friendly voice broke into their awestruck musings. "We're so glad you've joined us."

Check-in was quick and painless. As the receptionist handed them the keycard to their room, she shared a few helpful details.

"Percy will show you to your room and help with your luggage. We have you in the third-floor penthouse suite. We're hosting a private cocktail party this evening for the intel community, but you're welcome to mingle in the great room for wine and cheese. Our innkeeper will be on hand to visit with you and answer any questions you may have about your stay."

A jacketed man appeared behind them. "Let me take that for you," he said, taking Granny Bert's suitcase. Although Genny was no conventional beauty, he took one look into her sparkling blue eyes and dimpled smile and tripped over his own tongue. "Let me gets yours, too, ma'am. Miss. I'll be happy to show you around the inn, if you like." As an afterthought, he glanced back at Madison, left to trudge her own suitcase up all three flights of stairs. "I can come back for yours," he offered.

"There's no elevator?"

"Not yet."

"Never mind. I've got it." It shouldn't be much different than carrying laundry up to Bethani's third-floor bedroom, although her suitcase was heavier than she remembered. So much for packing light.

"As Chloe said, you ladies will be in the penthouse. It's my favorite, by the way," he said, his eyes dancing with intrigue. "You may not know it, but this home was patterned after a spy house in Germany during the Cold War. In the original house, operatives used this suite to watch the great room down below. It has mysterious spaces," he confided in a loud whisper.

When they reached the second floor, crossed through a cozy library, and started for the second staircase, Genny turned and took the suitcase from her friend. "Let me," she insisted. One tug, and she grunted. "Good grief, what did you pack in here?"

"I thought I was packing light," Madison said sheepishly. "I guess not."

"You may have to get behind me and push."

"Please," Percy interjected, "leave it and I'll bring it the rest of the way." He looked at Granny Bert. "Are you handling the stairs all right? We might have something available on a lower floor, although it won't be as large."

"Stand aside. I'll jog the rest of the way," the older woman said. Her huffed words had nothing to do with shortness of breath, but everything to do with injured pride.

"No offense, ma'am."

"None taken," she sniffed. "If you're through taking a breather, let's go."

Percy bit back a smile and led the women up the final flight of stairs, to the double doors just off the landing. "Your suite, ladies. Allow me." He reached for Genny's key card, allowing his fingers to brush against hers. With a flourishing hand movement, he threw open the doors and ushered them inside.

"This suite is almost as big as my entire house," Granny Bert exclaimed. "I may have to sleep in the hall to be closer to the bathroom."

The younger man laughed, not quite understanding the grain of truth behind her words. He pointed out a few highlights of the room and excused himself, but not before once again offering Genny a tour of the inn.

When he was gone, Madison placed her hand over

her heart and made a less-than-solemn vow. "I promise not to tell Cutter about your not-so-secret admirer. What happens at *Peralynna* stays at *Peralynna*."

Genny picked up a throw pillow from the sofa and lodged it at her friend. "Very funny."

"Hey, girls, get a load of these closets," Granny Bert said, wandering into the large space.

"There's supposed to be a loft in here somewhere," Genny said, wandering into the hall. She returned a few moments later to make her report. "There's another private deck out that way, and a narrow set of stairs that leads to a cozy little bedroom."

"I can take that one, if you like," Madison offered.

"Nah, I need the exercise more than you. Oh, and there's a half bath up there, too."

"There's a swimming pool in this bathroom," Granny Bert exaggerated. "These people must be in great physical shape, because there's more steps leading up to the tub. When you get up there, you can sink down and soak away the aches and pains of getting there." She shook her head with the irony.

"Why don't you two start unpacking while I check in with the contest organizers?" Genny suggested. "Then we can all go down and do some exploring."

Madison lifted their suitcases onto the proffered stands, grunting under the effort of her own bag. "I must have packed in my sleep, because I swear, I don't remember this being so heavy this morning," she muttered. She unzipped the basic black rolling bag and gasped. She rifled through the contents, not recognizing a single item. Most of it was folders, books, and ledgers. No wonder it was so heavy!

"I have someone else's luggage!" she stated with delayed realization.

"What are you mumbling about in here?" Granny

Bert asked, returning from the bathroom.

"I have the wrong suitcase! This isn't mine."

"How in tarnation did that happen?"

"I have no idea. Wait. The attendant stowed my luggage for me," she recalled. "I was one of the last people off the plane, which means that someone else mistook my luggage for theirs." She sank onto the side of the bed with a horrified sigh. "That means that *they* have mine, and I don't have a thing to wear!"

"Look on the bright side. You've needed a new wardrobe. Derron found you a few new pieces, but you still need a major update."

"Not like this, I don't! I don't even have a pair of underwear to change into."

"Relax, they have stores up here. There was a mall near the restaurant where we ate."

Madison continued to bemoan her troubles. "This is terrible, just terrible. My favorite boots were in that bag!"

"So call the airport, explain the mix-up, and see if the other person has already returned your bag. I'll bet it's there waiting on you."

"You're right. I should call the airport."

Her grandmother clicked her tongue. "What would you do without me? All this time, I thought I was the beauty and you were the brains, but maybe I was wrong. Maybe I've been both, all along."

In no mood for her grandmother's shenanigans, Madison already had her phone in her hand.

Three calls and an hour later, the news wasn't good. No one reported a missing suitcase, nor had they returned a piece of mistaken luggage. Without any identification on the bag in Madison's possession, they advised that she hang onto it until someone claimed it. Returning it to the airport could result in permanent loss.

"This is crazy. I can't believe they told me to just keep someone else's luggage!" Madison fumed.

"For all the good it does you. Nothing but a bunch of papers, from what I can tell. What little I read didn't even make sense," Granny Bert groused.

"I'm sure they told the other person to just keep mine, as well!" she continued to rant. "This is ridiculous."

"Let's find a store and buy you some new clothes, at least something for tonight and tomorrow," Genny suggested. "We'll come back, have a glass of wine, and call it a night. You can call the airport again in the morning. Even if no one has returned your suitcase, at least someone on the morning shift may be more helpful."

"They certainly can't be any more inept than the idiots working the phones this evening!"

"Calm down, Maddy. It's going to be fine." Genny stroked her friend's arms in a comforting gesture.

"You were right, you know. Something bad did happen." Madison threw her hands up in exasperation. "I lost all my underwear!"

Granny Bert snickered. "Somehow, I don't think Genny had a premonition about you losing your underwear."

"Go ahead. Laugh. Make a joke. It's fine for you. You have something to sleep in tonight."

"I know how you feel, you know," Genny said quietly. "I felt the same way when my house burned down. It's a terrible feeling, knowing you don't even own a fresh pair of panties or a toothbrush."

The comparison immediately quietened her friend. Maddy bit her lip in shame. "I'm sorry, Genny. Here I am, going on and on about a few lost items, things I packed for just a few days, when you lost literally everything. I should be ashamed for being so insensitive, and for overreacting the way I did."

"I didn't mean—"

"Of course you didn't," she broke in, silencing her friend with a hug. "It did me good to hear it, all the same. So. Let's go find a store and buy me some new threads." She slapped her hands together and grabbed her purse, which she knew was light on cash. She winced and added, "I may just have to shop at the dollar store. Things have been a little lean since Christmas." *Not to mention since Gray died and left me with all that debt, and hardly a dime to my name.*

"Nonsense. This will be my treat."

"Absolutely not!"

"I invited you along on this trip, and I'm the one who made us late this morning in the first place. It's my fault you lost your luggage."

"You had nothing to do with that major wreck on the interstate, or the fact my luggage has a twin and someone else took it by mistake."

"Still, I insist on buying, and I don't want to hear another word about it."

"No, Gen—"

"Nope, not another word. Think of it as an early trousseau present."

"I didn't buy you a trousseau present," Madison pointed out dryly.

With a giggle, Genny grabbed her own purse. "In that case, I'll buy my own. In fact, I'll treat us all three to a new outfit! Come on, ladies, let's go shopping!"


They returned with a half-dozen shopping bags.

Madison needed a little of everything. Other than a tube of lipstick and a comb she carried in her purse, she had no makeup, no hair products, and no change of clothes. The shoes she wore would do, even though their soles were slick on the icy pavement. Temperatures were typically colder here in Maryland than they were in Texas, and recent snowfall had melted and refrozen as a fine glaze of ice.

Though she might seldom wear it once she returned home, Madison chose a nice cable knit sweater in a rich moss green. The color looked good with her complexion and brought out tiny green flecks within her hazel eyes. The black slacks coordinated with the sweater and the second blouse Genny insisted on, a silky top of brilliant blue.

"I'll pay you back," Madison promised.

"Nonsense. I've been living with you since the fire, and you won't let me pay a dime for rent. Think of this as partial repayment for housing me all this time."

"Are you kidding? You do most of the cooking, not to mention the grocery shopping. It's better than having a live-in cook. You know Blake will go through withdrawals when you move out and he's stuck with my mediocre cooking again."

"I'll run these bags up and meet you back down here in a jiffy," Genny offered. "Like I said, I need the exercise."

"I can take them, or at least go with you."

"You stay and keep Granny Bert company." She flashed her dimpled smile and added, "Which we all know is code for keeping her out of trouble."

"I can hear you, you know," the older woman huffed.

Genny tossed a wink over her shoulder. "I know."

Madison and her grandmother wandered into the great room, where they found the wine and cheese bar. Helping themselves to the snacks and a glass of Chablis, they waited for Genny's return.

"All done?" Madison smiled when she saw her

friend. "Thanks for taking that up."

"No problem. Hey, how many other rooms are on our floor?"

"I think just that one suite, on the opposite end from ours."

"That's what I thought," Genny murmured.

"Why?"

"There was a guy up there, standing near our door when I came up. I can't be sure, but it looked like he was just hanging around our suite."

Madison shrugged. "Probably just nosy, hoping the door would open so he could get a peek inside. I've done the same thing myself a time or two," she said with a sheepish grin.

"You're probably right. Hey, did you see that I came down that staircase right over there, and not the front one? It will save us a few steps when we come down for breakfast in the morning."

"Now you sound like Blake, already thinking ahead to breakfast! I think my sixteen-year-old son is wearing off on you."

"It's true. I'm going to miss the kids when Cutter and I get married."

"I'll loan them to you anytime you need your food supplies depleted," Madison promised. Blake was at that magical age when he could eat the hinges off the door. It seemed impossible to fill his lanky form.

Sitting back to sip her wine, Madison watched the buzz of activity within the inn. Women in long, sequined gowns and glittering jewels arrived on the arm of four-star generals, foreign dignitaries, and politicians she recognized from the news. Discreet Secret Service agents stood along the perimeters, wearing earpieces and noticeable bulges beneath somber dinner jackets.

As quickly as the guests arrived, more agents

appeared and whisked them away to a secreted area. Each time the door fanned, Madison had a brief glimpse of sparkling champagne served in long, slender flutes, the twinkling lights of a grand chandelier, and the twirling images of silk and satin. The muted sounds of music and laughter drifted on the air, adding to the festive elegance of the ultra-private party.

"That must be quite a party in there," she guessed. "At least we know we're safe. With half the CIA and FBI here, you know the house is swarming with Secret Service."

"Not just the CIA. They don't call this the intel alphabet community for nothing, you know," Genny said. "Remember, I lived in DC for a few years, before moving to Boston. There's some sixteen or seventeen agencies that make up Intel and Homeland Security, most of them right in this area. CIA, FBI, NSA, DIA, DEA, NRO... I can't even begin to name them all."

"Angie from Annapolis said the same thing, but I didn't realize we were so close to the hotbed of activity," Madison murmured, her mind abuzz. Angie had said so much, it was difficult to retain half of it.

"The NSA is just down the road. And of course, the US Naval Academy is in Annapolis."

"I wonder if Mark Harmon is here tonight," Granny Bert asked, craning her neck as the front door opened. "That may be him, stepping out of that shiny black Maybach."

"Granny Bert, he's an actor, not an actual agent with the Navy," Genny reminded the older woman.

"I heard he researches for the part, to make it as authentic as possible. And that good-looking black guy over there looks a lot like the one who played Morgan on that show about the BAU. Isn't Quantico around here somewhere?"

While her companions debated the issue, Madison observed a tall, blond woman as she strode into the great room. Her first thought was that the woman was part of the intelligence community. She certainly carried herself with the confidence and air of authority needed in such a career. Or perhaps she was with the security team, Madison amended. The air around the woman fairly crackled with energy, even though she simply stood near the grand staircase, studying the entire room with one sweeping glance.

Madison's thoughts flashed to the beady-eyed man on the plane, the one who seemed perched on the edge of his seat, ready to pounce. *Two peas in a pod,* Maddy thought. Both full of suppressed energy.

If this woman was security, she was dressed differently from the others. No obvious earpiece, no bulge beneath her stylish navy blazer, just a soft alpaca European rolled turtleneck that brought out the blue of her eyes. Madison admired the thin gold bracelet on her wrist and the crystal pendant dangling from around her neck. Most of all, she admired the woman's smooth and steady gait as she gracefully exited the room, less than a minute after entering.

*A born athlete,* Madison mused. Despite being tall and lean herself, Maddy knew she lacked that special grace that came with athletic skills.

"I wonder if that was the innkeeper who just came through," she murmured, considering the possibility.

"Where? I didn't see anyone," Genny said.

"She came through that way—" Madison pointed to the area by the staircase "—stood there for a few seconds surveying the room, and went out that way. She was well dressed, but not fancy enough to be attending the party. She did look like someone important, though."

"According to their brochure, every guest here at

*Peralynna* is important." Genny smiled sweetly.

"What are you, their new advertising exec?" Granny Bert scoffed.

Genny shrugged her shoulders. "Hey, Maddy's letting Derron create an ad for *In a Pinch*. Maybe I want to do the same for this place. I've been reading up on it, and the more I read, the more fascinated I become."

Madison put her hand to her forehead. "Please, don't remind me about my hasty decision to give Derron more responsibility. Turning him loose while I'm gone may be the downfall of my business. The bright side is, it doesn't have far to fall."

To make ends meet after her husband died, Madison moved back to her hometown and started a temporary service. For the first several months, her staff of one—herself—filled in when clients were in a pinch and needed help. Derron Mullins had more or less appointed himself as her one and only part-time employee. When things were going well, she was even able to pay him.

"Maybe he'll find a dead body while we're gone and have you a new case to solve," Granny Bert chirped.

"Granny Bert, keep your voice down!" Madison hissed. "People here don't know you're kidding."

"Who's kidding? Since you came back to town, we've had a rash of dead bodies and crimes. Ronny Gleason, Caress Ellingsworth, that poor skeleton in the basement—"

"Okay, okay," Madison interrupted. "Point taken. But I had absolutely nothing to do with any of those."

"No, but you helped solve most of their cases," Genny said, obviously proud of her friend's investigative skills. In truth, she had a hand in solving most of them, as well. "Sometimes I think that's why

Brash is marrying you," she went on to tease. "That may be the only way our dear chief of police can control the town's up and coming new rogue investigator."

"I'm *not* a PI," Maddy reminded her with a groan. "I have a temporary work agency. Can I help it if people hire me to solve mysteries? And the main reason Brash can't solve them on his own is because his hands are tied by bureaucratic red tape and legal technicalities. And budget shortfalls," she added, remembering all the times he complained of limited funds. "Don't forget budget shortfalls and cuts."

"You know I'm just teasing. Brash is the best police chief either town has ever seen. We're lucky some big city hasn't already snatched him up and stolen him from us."

"It's not from lack of trying," Madison admitted. "He gets offers all the time, but he refuses them. He says he came back to raise Megan in the town he grew up in, and he has no plans of ever leaving again."

Her handsome fiancé had been away from the sister towns of Naomi and Juliet almost as long as she had. While Madison had married right out of college and settled in Dallas to start a family, Brash's career had been far more exciting. A football scholarship led to a brief career as a professional player, but he gave it up when his girlfriend came up pregnant. His turbulent marriage only lasted until Megan was a toddler, but Brash had gone on to coach at several premier colleges in Texas, reluctant to stray far from his daughter. Eventually giving up the sport completely—other than hosting summer camps for underprivileged youths—Brash studied law enforcement and returned to The Sisters to serve as father to Megan and chief of police to the small community. Without the bindings of romance, he and ex-wife Shannon had become close friends. She was now married to his best friend and together, the three of them were raising a wonderful young woman, who just happened to be best friends with Madison's daughter.

"That man has a good head on his shoulders," Granny Bert remarked. "He can't be swayed with inflated salaries and strokes to his ego. You did good, finally snagging that man after all these years."

It was no secret that Madison had a crush on him in high school, but it had taken twenty years to discover he reciprocated her feelings. She could never think of the years as wasted, however, no matter how unhappy her marriage had become before Gray's sudden death. After all, she had Bethani and Blake during that time, and Brash had Megan. She already loved the auburn-haired teen as her own, and Brash, in turn, adored the twins. Blake had a special bond with the lawman that had been missing with his biological father. It warmed Madison's heart every time she saw the two of them together.

"If he ever leaves the department, the two of you could start your own detective agency," Genny suggested.

"But I thought you and I were going to start one," Madison teased. "What was that name you came up with? *Soup and Snoop.* Lunch and investigation services, all in one handy stop."

"But then you went and gave up your corner booth at the café, and got that snazzy new office in the remodel," Genny pretended to pout. "No soup compares with that."

"No, but your Gennydoodle cookies do." Madison pushed away her half-eaten chocolate chip cookie with a sigh. "Honestly, after eating your desserts, nothing else comes close. How are you going to judge that contest tomorrow, knowing your own creations are ten times better?"

Genny's laugh was modest. "It's good for me to keep up with the competition. Don't get me wrong, I love what I do and where I'm at, but my customers don't exactly know the difference between chocolate ganache and chocolate mousse. And Cutter, bless his heart, is content with nothing but apple turnovers for the rest of his life, with an occasional tiramisu thrown in on special occasions. I need a reminder now and then of how the other half lives. Or bakes."

"Keep it simple, girl, and you'll never go wrong," her stand-in grandmother advised. They weren't blood related, but they were family, nonetheless.

"Speaking of tomorrow, I asked, but unfortunately, you can't come with me. I'm afraid you and Granny Bert will have to find some other way to entertain yourselves."

"That's no problem. I'm sure there's plenty to do around here. Isn't that right, Granny?"

Her grandmother nodded with enthusiasm. "I saw a brochure in the lobby, something about a zip line near here. You know I love to zip line."

"It may be too cold, but we'll check it out," Madison promised. A frown creased her forehead. "And you're right. We have vastly different ideas of fun."

"You know what they say. To each her own. You can stand around and watch paint dry, while I whisk my way through the treetops." Her grandmother used a wave of her bony hand for emphasis.

"Oh, look," Genny broke in, "I bet that's the innkeeper. She was just visiting with those people at the table, and now she's moving this way. She seems to be working her way through the room."

Soon, a pleasant-looking, sixty-something woman

made her way into the sunken sitting room where they were. "Hello," she said with a warm smile. "I'm Sophie Jamison, your innkeeper. Welcome to *The Columbia Inn at Peralynna*."

As the three women introduced themselves, Sophie helped herself to a seat on the sofa next to Genny. "What brings you to our area?"

"I'm judging a benefit cooking competition this week. My friends came along to make it a girl's trip."

"How delightful! Is that the competition being held at *Fretz Kitchens*? Someone called yesterday about possibly having one segment of the contest filmed here. I think it depends upon how the judging goes, and whether there's a tie. What a wonderful coincidence that you're staying here!"

"It would certainly be convenient for me," Genny agreed with a twinkle in her eye.

The innkeeper wagged her finger as recognition dawned in her face. "Wait a minute. I know you ladies! You're from Texas and did that television show about restoring an old mansion. You're the one with the café. You make some sort of fabulous apple turnovers, if that good-looking firefighter is to be believed."

Blushing in spite of herself, Genny laughed and admitted, "I certainly hope so. We're getting married on Valentine's Day."

"Married? Congratulations! How exciting!"

"This trip doubles as her bachelorette party," Madison told the other woman.

"That's right," Granny Bert pitched in. "Know any fun spots where we can take her for a good time?"

Sophie laughed, wagging her finger again at the elderly woman. "Ah, I remember you, Granny Bert. Always a live one, you are!"

"It's how I keep young."

"I loved your television show, by the way. It often made me think of this house. You're not the only one with hidden passages and secret staircases, you know. This house has quite a few of its own."

"We read something about that," Madison said, "but we'd love to hear more."

"The owner's parents were CIA agents back in the day, and apparently having children was the perfect cover for covert missions and clandestine meetings. After all, who would question a family outing? It appeared completely innocent. The owner remembers having grand parties and overnight guests in a house just like this one in Germany, near the Taunus Mountains. It wasn't until she was much older that she realized her parents were operatives, and that many of their guests were spies, and quite often dangerous."

"We're in the penthouse, and I understand that in the original house, it was used to watch over the rest of the house. Is that correct?"

"Yes, I believe so." Sophie nodded. She twisted so that she could point out the row of windows on both the third and fourth tiers of the massive room. "You see those windows that wrap around there on the third floor? Those are in your room, and from there, you have excellent views. You can even see onto the decks outside, and into the edge of the kitchen. The fourth floor connects to your room, as well, and spills into the loft you see. We use it for storage now, but when this was a private home, it was a wonderful reading room and play area for the owners' grandchildren."

"I see many similarities to the Big House," Madison nodded.

"We even have a basement," Sophie said, her eyes twinkling. "However, we encourage guests to explore ours. We have a wonderful pool table down there, as well as several suites."

"No secret passages down to a hidden room?" Granny Bert asked.

In reply, Sophie merely smiled. "I'll never tell."

Genny leaned forward. "So where are the secret staircases?"

"If I told you that, they wouldn't be secret, now would they?"

"Do they go up, or down?"

Sophie paused for a moment before divulging that small bit of information. "Both."

"You know you have our curiosity up now," Madison told her, her tone a bit reproachful.

"Exactly. And you are welcome to explore the inn and do your best to locate all of our intriguing spaces. As long as the door isn't locked or marked as private, you are welcome to explore."

"That doesn't sound like most hotels I've ever been to," Genny said.

"Because *The Columbia Inn at Peralynna* isn't your ordinary hotel," Sophie was quick to say. "Remember, this is a home."

Madison looked beyond the sunken alcove where they sat, to an interesting recess next to the staircase. "What's that little nook?"

"We call it the Cuddle Room, because it has that comfy little settee where you can cuddle up with a good book or a loved one. But in the original house, it served as a card room. I understand there was a curtain covering the arch. As gambling was illegal, the tables were built into the walls. With the touch of a lever, the walls folded down to expose card tables and chairs. Otherwise, they were hidden in plain sight."

Granny Bert was fascinated with the revelation. "Sounds a bit like a get-up we had back in Prohibition

Days, when I was running moonshine."

"Granny!" Madison chided, but her grandmother sent her a simmering look.

"I told you, child, times were hard, and we did what we had to do to get by. I was proud to be a bootlegger, and a darned good one, at that. I wasn't any older than that little hellion that bumped into me at the airport today, but I helped put food on my family's table."

"She wasn't a hellion, Granny, she was a sweet little girl who gave me a drawing."

Sophie arched a graying brow. "At the airport?"

Madison did an airy wave with her fingers. "It was nothing, just a simple little flower, done in crayon."

"You had me worried there for a moment," Sophie admitted with a small laugh. "Being so close to Washington and Fort Meade, and with so many stories of espionage and spy secrets surrounding this house, I suppose I often let my imagination get the better of me."

"Does the owner ever tell you stories from her childhood?"

"Oh, yes. I can sit and listen to her for hours. Did you know there was a recent blockbuster movie that included a real-life incident involving her father and one of their more famous guests? You can read more about it in an article we have framed in the hallway. And there's the National Cryptologic Museum just a few miles from here that has an exact replica of the bugged Great Seal, which is also tied to the story. You should definitely check it out."

"We will," Madison said. "Granny and I need something to do while Genny is busy judging the competition."

Genny offered her trademark dimpled smile. "Hey, it's a tough job, but someone's gotta do it!"

Sophie visited with them for another twenty minutes, sharing a few of the spy stories she was familiar with. By the time she wished them a good evening, her guests were feeling the buzz of a good mystery.

"I'm so glad we chose this hotel," Genny said, her voice filled with excitement. "I mean, I'm sorry about the other hotel burning down, but it turned out for the best, as far as we're concerned. Who knew a place like this even existed?"

They took fresh nightcaps up to their room, and Granny Bert carried a plate of crackers and grapes. They took the back stairway, which brought them directly into the library.

"Sophie told us to help ourselves to a book or a DVD," Genny said, noting the many choices scattered about on multiple bookcases.

"I don't know about you girls, but I'm plumb tuckered out." For once, Granny Bert openly admitted her exhaustion.

"To tell you the truth, so am I. Not that way, Granny Bert." When the older woman would have crossed the room and gone down the hallway on the other side, Maddy gently took her arm and directed her to make a sharp right. "This way."

"This house has too many angles and turns," the older woman complained. "I thought we went that way."

She jerked a thumb over her shoulder as she started up the narrow staircase. A bit confused herself, Madison looked again, just to make certain they were in the right place. She got a glimpse of a man in a black jacket as he disappeared around the corner. She waited for the sound of a door to shut but heard nothing. She shot Genny a curious glance. "Where did that guy go?" she whispered.

"Hold on a sec," Genny said. She dashed across the room and peeked around the corner. She hurried back with a giggle. "Good grief, there's another set of stairs going down on that side! This place is like a maze."

"Just point me in the direction of my bed," Granny Bert grumbled.

"Up. Up, up, up."

An hour and a half later, Granny Bert snored softly beneath the downy covers, Genny soaked alone in a tub made for two, and Maddy ended her call to Brash, a melancholy smile upon her face. She'd been gone for less than one day, but simply knowing they were fifteen hundred miles apart made her miss him that much more.

She unfolded her long form from the sofa and moved to the wall of windows overlooking the great room below. Floor-to-ceiling drapes offered more than adequate privacy. She might never have pushed the drapes aside, had she not known what lay beyond.

Madison stood well behind the curtains, afraid someone down below might see her in her new nightgown. Genny chose it for her, saying that after this trip, she could tuck it away for her honeymoon. Why buy a boring flannel gown, her friend reasoned, when Brash would much prefer this one? If she shared a room with anyone other than her grandmother and her very best friend, Maddy would never have agreed, but over the years, both women had seen her in less clothes than this. And she had to admit, the delicate fabric felt heavenly against her skin, even if it was scandalously thin. At least Granny lent her an extra robe, even though it didn't do her much good now, hanging in the bathroom where Genny took her bath.

Parting the drapes ever so slightly, Madison

peered out through the opening. She almost felt guilty, like she was spying on the people down below. Which, she supposed, was the whole idea behind the room in the first place. For all she knew, they might have some sort of one-way glass, but she didn't want to take any chances. She would simply take a peek.

No one stirred below. The lights in the great room were dimmed and the house, it appeared, was sleeping.

Sophie was right. Madison had an excellent view of the room below, even with the lighting turned low. From here, she could easily see into the sunken parlor where they sat earlier, entertained with Sophie's third-party tales of espionage and intrigue. She smiled as a thrill of excitement raced through her, even now. The innkeeper certainly knew how to tell an enchanting tale.

Madison was about to drop the curtain when movement from below caught her eye. She saw a man moving through the shadows, crossing from the sunken parlor into the kitchen area. Something told her he wasn't an employee of the hotel. His movements were too stealthy, his manner too guarded. He stopped more than once, glancing around to make certain no one saw him, but he failed to look up, toward the soaring ceiling and the wall of windows. After a moment of nosing about, the man crossed the room and Madison lost sight of him. She could never see his face, but she thought he wore a black jacket, like the man exiting the library when they came up.

Coincidence, she assured herself. Again, she almost turned away, until she discovered that the huge mirror above the fireplace offered a perfect view of the staircase directly across from it. She could only see the bottom four or five steps, but it was enough to watch how the man hesitated there, apparently still checking his surroundings, before finally continuing to the second floor.

"Maddy?" Genny called softly, padding into the room in her bare feet. "What are you doing?"

Madison dropped the curtain as if it suddenly stung her fingers. "N—Nothing," she denied guiltily.

"Then why do you look like you just got caught with your hand in Granny Bert's cookie jar?"

With a sheepish smile, Madison motioned to the sofa. Careful not to wake her sleeping grandmother, she kept her voice low as she curled onto the cushions.

"I know it's silly. I think I got caught up in Sophie's stories earlier. She knows how to tell a tale, doesn't she?"

"She certainly does," Genny agreed, tucking her legs beneath her on the other side of the couch. "The whole time I was in the tub, I thought about what she told us. Can you imagine living that life? Full of spies and secrets, and never knowing when someone might be listening in on your conversations?"

"I know all about that, remember?" Madison said, shivering with the memory of when her own house was bugged. During the filming of the reality show, certain areas of their home were strictly off limits, but a devious cameraman had his own agenda, and hid mics without their knowledge.

"True. But you still didn't tell me why you looked so guilty when I came in. Don't tell me there's a speaker in here and you can hear everything they're saying below!"

"The lights are out and there's no one below. Well, there was one guy... Again, I'm sure it was my imagination, but he seemed to be... snooping."

Genny sat up straight. "Like the man I saw earlier, outside our room?"

Madison scowled. "I forgot about that. Do you remember what he was wearing?"

"Uh… a jacket, maybe? Navy? Maybe black. I'm not sure."

Unease skittered across Madison's nerves. "There was also that man on the second floor, when we were coming up. He had on a black jacket. And so did the man downstairs just now."

"Along with thousands of other people. It's like thirty-five degrees outside, you know. Most people are wearing jackets."

"I know. You're absolutely right." Madison rubbed her fingers against her forehead. "Like I said, I'm sure it's just my over-active imagination. I got a little too caught up in listening to Sophie's stories. Forget I said anything."

"How can I? You're not the one sleeping all alone in that loft. According to Sophie, it may or may not have a hidden space or two, itself."

"I'll take the loft," Madison offered. "Better yet, I'll take this couch, and you can crawl in bed with Granny."

"Your long legs wouldn't fit. *I'll* take the couch." Genny rooted down into the cushions, demonstrating how she was the perfect fit. "Snug as a bug in a rug."

"You sure?"

"Absolutely! I'm so tired I could probably sleep on the floor."

Madison scooted off the couch and smiled. "You and me both. You have a big day tomorrow, so you'd better get some sleep."

"The studio is sending a car for me, so that leaves you and Granny Bert with the Lincoln. I'll probably be gone most of the day."

"Just as long as we have time for a nice dinner together. This is your bachelorette trip, after all, and you need a little time for some fun."

"A nice dinner sounds great."

"I'll find you a blanket."

"Oh, and tomorrow night? We'll skip the spy tales and I'll be a big girl and sleep in my own bed," Genny promised.

Madison only laughed. "Sounds like a plan."

# 5

Madison slept soundly, too exhausted to worry about spies and men in dark jackets.

By morning, she saw no shadows down below. When she peeked from their draperies by the light of day, bright sunshine greeted her. It poured down from a dozen skylights, streamed in through dual sets of French doors, flooded in from all directions to drench the bright and airy space. The temperatures outside might be cold, but the sun shone brightly on this early February day.

Several people milled about in the great room, having breakfast at the scattered tables below. A young couple had an animated conversation over eggs and toast, while a businessman studied his computer between gulps of coffee. Another woman carried a plate piled high with pastries and danishes and deposited it beside her husband, who kept his face buried in the morning newspaper. Madison saw no sign of a man wearing a black jacket.

"Silliness on my part," she scoffed, dropping the curtain.

"What's that?" her grandmother asked from the closet.

"Just wondering if you were ready for breakfast."

"Two more minutes, a visit to the little girl's room, and I'm good to go. Airplanes always do a number on my bladder."

"No hurry. We have the whole day."

While her grandmother finished getting ready, Madison called home.

"*In a Pinch Professional Services.* This is Derron speaking. How may I connect your call?"

Without preamble, Madison launched in. "I've been gone exactly one day! Please tell me you didn't install a new phone system!"

The man's cool professional tone dissolved into a delighted squeal. "Hey, dollface, how's the big city?"

"A bit chilly. But you didn't answer my question."

"That's because I didn't hear a question. But in the interest of speeding this conversation along, no, I didn't put in a new phone system. Nice touch, though, jazzing up my greeting like that, don't you think? Makes us sound more high class."

"Good thing, too, since our last client wanted us to locate his lost pig," Madison muttered.

"Those days may be behind us, dollface. Our ad came out this morning, and we've already had two callers."

"Seriously?"

"Okay, so one of them thought the *In a Pinch* referenced cooking measurements and wanted to know how many cups there were to a pound of lard, but the other was a solid lead. We may have a client needing clerical services for a ten-week maternity leave."

Madison was still hung up on the lard reference. "Who uses lard these days? Have they never heard of clogged arteries?"

"Apparently not. She wanted to put it in her

grandmother's recipe for cracklin' cornbread and serve it with deep fried bacon and fried green tomatoes."

"Southern to the core," Madison murmured.

"Be careful what you say, madam. You're in Yankee territory now," Derron teased, using an exaggerated accent.

When enemy lines and Union spies came to mind, Madison feared she was still under the spell of Sophie's stories from the night before. "So how does the ad look?" she asked, determined to forget such nonsense.

"Like a million bucks." She could just imagine her part-time employee's mega-watt smile. Derron had a flair for the dramatics, but the man was good at most anything he did. Designing an ad should be no different. "Which, by the way, is roughly what it cost. I may have misread the cost sheet," he said with a sudden rush of words.

"Derron! I gave you a strict budget! You know we can't afford anything extravagant. We can't even afford anything cheap," she wailed. "I knew this was a mistake."

"Relax, dollface. They agreed to run it a second week for free, so we're getting twice the exposure."

"This ad better bring in business, Derron," she warned sternly. "That was money I was saving for Bethani's cheerleading camp. If she gets kicked off the squad, it's on you."

"Oops, getting a call. Gotta go," the young man said. "Probably someone calling from the ad. Bye, love you, be safe." The line went dead before Madison had a chance to reply.

"I didn't hear any beep," she muttered, staring at her phone in suspicion. "He just didn't want to get chewed out."

Granny Bert breezed into the room, hearing only the last part of the conversation. "And who would? Come on, girl, let's go chew on some breakfast."

"*In a Pinch Temporary Services.* This is Derron, how may I direct your call?"

"I saw your ad in the paper," a man's gruff voice said. "Put someone on who can help me."

"Certainly, sir. One moment please."

Derron tapped the *hold* button and continued browsing his social media feed, snickering when he saw a cute meme posted by a friend. He sang a bar of his new favorite pop song and waited for what he felt was an appropriate amount of time, before depressing the *hold* button.

"I'm so sorry for the wait, sir. We're experiencing an extremely high number of calls this morning. Perhaps I can help you. What sort of services were you in need of?"

The man hesitated, obviously debating on how to proceed. Decision made, his voice rumbled with the rough edge of emotion. "I need help with my daughter. I think she's fallen in with the wrong crowd."

"Yes, I see," Derron said. Good thing the caller couldn't see the way his brow puckered in pure confusion. "How exactly can we help you, sir?"

"Well, I thought you could follow her and see what she's up to. My wife died a couple of years ago, and the girl won't talk to me. Now she has all these new friends, and she won't bring 'em round the house. Says she's *ashamed* of the place. Maybe it ain't a palace, but it's the best I can do, you know? Do you know what it's like, raising a smart-mouthed sixteen-year-old girl, all by yourself?" the man grumbled.

"No, sir, I certainly don't," Derron commiserated. His voice brightened as he added, "But I have recently acquired a parrot, and I know how difficult it is to raise a smart-mouthed bird."

"Uh, well, that's not really the same thing," the man stuttered. "Unless your parrot started wearing black nail polish and baggy clothes."

"No, his claws are painted light blue, same as mine," Derron answered, glancing down at his feet. He couldn't see the results of his latest pedicure through the canvas uppers, but he knew the color was perfect for his skin tone. It didn't look half bad on his colorful bird, either. "I'd love to hear more about your daughter, sir."

"Like what?"

"Her name, her hobbies, where she goes to school, what she likes to do. That sort of thing."

"Oh, right. Uhm, her name is Tasha. She's a sophomore at Riverton High. Good student. At least, I guess she still is. No teachers have called to say different."

*That could be the problem right there*, Derron thought, but he wisely kept his mouth shut. Obviously, the dad wasn't involved enough in his daughter's life.

"What does Tasha like to do?"

"She used to have friends, but now all she does is play on that dad-blamed phone all the time. When we get a chance to eat together, I made a rule, no phone at the dinner table. So, she quit coming to the table. Stopped leaving notes about where she was going and what time she'd be back."

"How old did you say she was, sir?" The frown bled through his words.

"Sixteen."

He couldn't resist. "And *she* tells *you* what time

she'll be home?"

Properly chastised, the man was quiet before offering a rumbled excuse. "You gotta understand. I work two jobs, just so she can have that phone and those new baggy clothes."

The man's plight reaffirmed what Derron already suspected.

It was far easier to parent a bird, than a child.

# 6

After breakfast, Madison and Granny Bert headed off to the National Cryptologic Museum. Particularly after talking to Derron, it helped knowing the museum was free to the public and within her limited budget.

Brash, of course, repeatedly offered to help her with her finances, but Madison was determined to maintain her independence. For almost twenty years, she had entrusted her family's financial security to her husband, and look where that had gotten her. Unbeknownst to her, Grayson bankrupted their investment company, 'misappropriated' some of their clients' funds, took a second mortgage on a house they couldn't afford in the first place, borrowed from his life insurance policy to support his mistress, and then had the gall to die before he faced the consequences of his reckless actions. That deed had fallen upon his widow and two children. Madison knew Brash deCordova was an honorable man and would never deceive her so, but it was important she learn to stand on her own. She *needed* to provide for her family. The twins deserved as much.

"Look here," Granny Bert said, stopping at the first exhibit. "These are hobo symbols. Back in the day—*way* back in the day—folks depended on the goodness of others when they were down on their luck. They didn't depend on government handouts and programs that pay you to sit home on your rumpus instead of going out and earning an honest day's wages. Back in those days, when you needed a little boost, you asked your neighbor. And if you were the traveling sort, going from town to town to find work, you looked to the kindness of strangers. These symbols let the next traveler know where he could find a hot meal or a bed for the night. See that? That cat symbol means a kind lady lives there."

Madison was wise enough not to mention some of the other symbols. Two rectangles, one with a zig-zag bottom, meant the owner would give to get rid of you. The simple "+" sign with three dots inside a circle meant the doctor wouldn't charge for his services. An X inside a circle meant it was a good place for a hand-out. The only difference Madison could see in then and now was that these days, the government paid for the handouts, and it was no longer considered begging. Some called it progress.

They wandered through the hallways, learning more about deciphering codes. Because the museum was part of the National Security Agency, the information was geared toward codes as they pertained to the nation's defense.

"I seldom get to see the Civil War through the eyes of the North," Madison mused, as they wandered into the section devoted to the battle between the states.

"Most folks think it was only about slavery, but that was just part of it. The North didn't like the Southern states getting so powerful. Truth is, the war was more about politics, big machinery, and the manufacturing plants in the North, than it was about freeing slaves. Sure, there were some abolitionists in it for the right reasons, but like any smart politician, bigwigs knew to get the fanatics involved. Find someone passionate enough to lobby their cause, and you can ride in on their coattails. Mark my words, many a crooked agenda has ridden in under the guise of a good cause."

"But slavery was wrong," Madison said.

"Absolutely. It's not like all Southerners owned slaves, you know. Most folks didn't have enough money to support their own families, much less slaves. Most Southerners fought for their way of life in general, not for the right to own another person." Granny Bert snorted her disapproval. "They forget to teach that in history class these days."

"Actually, they don't teach about the Civil War at all. Which is really sad, because how can we learn from our mistakes, if we pretend they never happened?"

"Politics, child. Stick your head in the sand and hope the problem goes away."

They wandered further into the museum, coming to the exhibit on Early Cryptography and the infamous Enigma machine.

"Fascinating," Granny Bert acknowledged. "The Germans thought this fancy code of theirs couldn't be broken. Even now, it looks complicated, with all those rotors and keys. Imagine what they thought of that technology in the 1920s!"

"I guess that's why it took so long to break it," Madison agreed, reading the placards around the legendary machine. "You have to admit, that was a pretty sophisticated system. No wonder they called it the Enigma."

Granny Bert pointed to a staggering statistic on the

wall. "Look at how many possible combinations it created. I've never seen a number that long. It took three mathematicians, but they finally deciphered it." She glanced over her shoulder and continued, keeping her voice low. "And don't look now, but I think you have an admirer. Although these days, it might be called a stalker."

Naturally, Madison looked around. "What are you talking about?"

"That guy over there, the one standing behind that cabinet. He keeps watching you. Followed us all through the Cold War and the Vietnam jungle."

"I don't see anyone. Are you sure it's not a mannequin?"

"You think my eyes are going, along with my bladder?" her grandmother huffed. "Believe me, no one would make a mannequin that ugly. Bulb nose, beady eyes, intense gaze."

Madison stiffened at the mention of a stalker. Something about Granny Bert's description—bulb nose, intense gaze—stirred an image in her mind, but she couldn't quite place it. Probably some gangster in a movie, she decided, forcing herself to relax. They were, after all, once again on the subject of spies.

"I still don't see anyone," Madison whispered, but it wasn't from lack of trying. If someone was there, he was invisible.

"I don't know where he went, but for a while there, I could have sworn he was following us."

"It is a rather small museum," she pointed out, trying to convince herself along with her grandmother. "We keep seeing that same mother and son, and that sweet Hispanic couple from Kansas."

"I thought they said they were from Kentucky. He had on a Jack Daniels t-shirt."

Madison resisted rolling her eyes. "Which means

absolutely nothing. They sell their whiskey everywhere, you know."

"Speaking of whiskey, where are we taking Genny this evening? It's not a bachelorette party if you don't get the bride a little tipsy."

"I don't recall you being so open-minded when I was the bride."

"That was different. You were little more than a child. That, and the fact *I* wasn't invited."

"Imagine that," Maddy teased. "A young bride not wanting to invite her grandmother to her bachelorette party. How rude of me."

"Darn tootin' it was rude! I could have told you all you needed to know about the wedding night, and then some."

Madison cupped her hands over her ears and vigorously shook her head. "No, not this again! *Please* don't tell me how Grandpa Joe invented sex."

Her grandmother gave a mournful shake of her own gray head. "I sure miss that man."

Desperate to change the subject, Maddy tugged the older woman forward. "Moving along now. Let's see what the *Power of Purple* is."

"You're too young to know, but I remember my father and uncle talking about this from World War II. The Purple Cipher, they called it, or the Purple Code. Like the Enigma, it was very sophisticated for its day. The US actually cracked the code before Pearl Harbor and could have prepared for the attack, but for some reason, our side didn't heed the warnings. You know how *that* turned out."

"It looks like the Japanese also used a changing rotor system, with a different key each day." Madison scanned the placards that told the story behind breaking the code. "Something about sixes and twenties, so I guess it used numbers, as well."

"No," her grandmother corrected, "the sixes were the five vowels and Y. The twenties were the consonants. And it says here the expert working on the case suffered a mental breakdown and was institutionalized. So, the poor guy's job literally drove him crazy."

"Can you imagine doing all this by hand, before computers? No wonder he had a breakdown. There were a gazillion possibilities."

"What's the possibility of us getting out of here before lunch?"

"Just a few more exhibits and we're done."

Granny Bert visibly brightened. "Then we'll go check out the zip lines?"

"Yes, Granny, then we'll go check out the zip lines."

# 7

"What was this place? I love the architecture," Madison said, peering at the massive brick structure before them.

"Looks like an old cotton gin, but I thought that was a Southern thing."

"Technically, Maryland *is* a Southern state, you know."

"Uptown South," Granny Bert harrumphed. "Notice this gin is made of bricks, when all of ours are made of tin." Back home in The Sisters, the old cotton gin had been converted into a Fire Station and occasional party room, tin and all.

"Still, it's very interesting. This must have been an entire complex, with a mill and weaving rooms and everything!"

"Good use of the space," the older woman acknowledged, "turning it into an antique mall with shops and businesses. Not to mention a zip line, somewhere around here."

"I would assume that would be at the top."

"So, what are we waiting for? Let's go to the top."

Madison followed her grandmother down the long sidewalk and through the doors. "Where do you get your energy? I'm half your age and I swear, I only have half your energy."

"For one thing, I don't waste energy on things I can't change. For another, I don't waste sleeping time on worrying. When I go to bed at night, I hand my troubles over to the good Lord. I figure He's going to be up all night, anyway."

Madison made no comment, simply walked beside the wise older woman on their journey to the top floor.

Their climb was in vain.

"Closed? Closed! We come all this way up here, and they're closed?" Granny Bert cried in disappointment.

"I suppose it is winter time. They have to consider the safety of their clients during snow and ice season."

"The sun is shining and it's almost forty degrees out here! It's colder than this at home today, and you don't see Texas closed!"

"Just like Maryland isn't closed," Madison rationalized, much as she would to a child. "But this particular business is. Again, a safety precaution."

Her grandmother made a few noises of protest, but she settled down. "At least it's a pretty view," she said.

"I'll bet it's gorgeous when the trees are budded out and all green. Or in the fall, when the leaves turn orange and gold." They looked around for several minutes, admiring the scenery and the Little Patuxent River that ran alongside the old mill. They imaged a time when a water wheel churned in the free-flowing energy source. All that was left now was a crumbling shell of a building.

After a while, Madison turned her attention to the beauty of the building's interior.

"Look at those massive beams. It's amazing to think how they used to mill these and lift them in place, without the help of modern-day machinery.

And look up there. It still has all the old pulleys and wheels."

"It's a cool old place, even if the best part of it is closed for the season," Granny Bert agreed.

They took a set of metal steps down, lingering at a store filled with antique furniture and nick knacks.

"I love this place. But I see some dangerous spots, too," Madison observed. "Look out that window. There's a cute little courtyard, but no way to access it. What if someone fell into it? And did you see how steep that ground was down to the river?"

Granny Bert laughed at her critique. "You've definitely been trapped too many times, child, if you look at this place and see only the danger."

"Maybe," Madison agreed. "But, still. That courtyard had no way out. Neither does that big grassy spot down there with all the pipes. You could fall right in."

"That's what the rails are for, to keep fools from falling—or jumping—down there. And if the courtyard was fully enclosed, there may not have been a way out, which means there was also no way in. That's another one of my tricks for having so much energy. Always think of the glass as half full, not half empty." While she was spouting life lessons, she threw in another. "And remember, it takes more face muscles to frown, than it does to smile."

A few moments later, Madison pointed out that her grandmother used unnecessary energy by frowning.

"We're several miles from where we were earlier, right?"

"I think we might be a town or so over. Why?"

"Don't look now—and I mean it, *don't. look*—but that same guy is still following us."

Madison bit her lip and resisted the urge to twist

her head. "Are you sure it's him?"

"Unless God made an awful mistake and created two of those faces, I'm positive."

"Where is he?"

"Behind us. I'll pretend to stop and look at something, and you can sneak a peek." Without warning, her grandmother veered sharply to the left.

"Would you look at that gorgeous top!" she exclaimed, pointing to quite possibly the ugliest blouse Madison had ever seen. While Granny Bert fawned over the wild combination of colors and patterns, Madison managed a glimpse of the man who took a sudden interest in an antique vase, one store behind them.

She couldn't see his face, but she felt his eyes upon her.

"I think we should go back to the hotel," Madison murmured. "Now."

"Right behind you," Granny Bert said, but not before creating a diversion. As she turned, her foot snagged the foot of the metal mannequin displaying the blouse. It toppled over with a clatter, taking a slender glass case with it when it fell. Glass splintered in every direction. A long necklace hanging with the blouse broke and scattered, spilling colorful beads across the floor of the mall.

"Hurry!" Granny Bert urged, pushing Madison forward.

They rushed from the scene, not waiting to see the full extent of the damages. As they hit the door, Madison glanced back. The man who had been following them had no choice but to stay behind, caught in the wake of Granny Bert's destruction.

# 8

"Thanks for coming over, Cutter. Take a load off."

Brash indicated the chairs facing his semi-cluttered desk. Two precarious stacks of files and folders made a haphazard climb upward, more or less contained within neatly aligned metal baskets. The calendar-style desk blotter sported coffee stains and a smear of mustard, but all notes and appointments were written in a neat, bold, masculine hand. Judging from the way the forty-three-year-old rested his arms on the scarred but solid desk, he was comfortable in the semi-clutter. And in his role as The Sisters' chief of police.

The men shook hands before the firefighter took a seat. "How's it going today?" Cutter asked.

"I think I've finally mastered Maddy's fancy cooktop. We made it through the rest of breakfast without any major mishaps. Sorry about the false alarm."

"Hey, I like my bacon with a crispy crunch. They say a little charcoal is good for you, anyway," the fire chief said with a grin.

"The black bacon didn't bother Blake, but both girls turned up their noses at it. They suddenly decided they were on a diet."

"Is that why they stopped by *Ngo's Donuts* on the way to school?"

"Something like that." Brash chuckled.

"So how are the four of you making it, rambling around in that big old house?"

"I don't think I ever realized how big that house really is, until I spent the first night in it. Just securing it for the night was a workout in itself."

"That's what the electronic alarm system is for," Cutter pointed out. He knew fully well that Brash preferred a more manual, hands-on sort of security, same as him.

"Never hurts to be sure." Brash leaned back in his chair and studied the other man. The custom leather creaked beneath his weight, masking a similar protest from his knee. Years of playing football, from flag to pro, had a way of doing that to a body. "So what brings you in, Cutter? You said you had something to share."

Almost ten years separated them in age, but the men had become good friends. Between their prospective careers and the women they loved, their lives often intersected. It wasn't unusual for either man to drop in unannounced on the other, but today, Cutter had called ahead. This was business.

"I got the official report back from the state fire marshal on that blaze over on Old Tap Road. Just as we suspected. Arson."

"Can't say it comes as any surprise."

"No, but it seems to have a lot of similarities to the fire at Harold Beavey's old barn. And to a couple of empty houses on the outskirts of Riverton."

The lawman's sigh was heavy. "We get rid of one meth operation, and two more pop out. A lot like gray hairs."

Cutter couldn't help but rub in the age difference. "I wouldn't know about that," he said with a sly grin. When his friend arched his brow in his trademark smirk, the younger man gave an innocent shrug. "Blond hair, you know."

He dropped the cocky attitude as he leaned forward and spoke in all sincerity. "I don't think they're cooking meth. I think they're practicing."

Clearly surprised, Brash's tone was cautious. "For what?"

"Something bigger."

"You gotta give me more than that, Montgomery."

"I've done a little poking around. With each fire, the mark gets bigger. A two-house shack to a rambling old farmstead. A large barn. Now an office building at an oilfield. I'm worried about what may be next."

Brash considered his words as he toyed with a pen. "What are you thinking?"

"From all indications, this is the work of a group of kids. But make no mistake. This isn't a secret boy's club with an inept Keeper of the Flame. Each fire becomes more sophisticated, more daring. More deliberate."

"Any clues as to who they are?"

"No, but I do know we're dealing with a group of smart, derelict, misguided kids who have a problem with authority and constructive curriculum."

Worry settled upon Brash's face. "You think they'll target a school."

"I have no concrete evidence to back it up," Cutter admitted. "But, yeah. That's what my gut tells me."

Brash blew out a deep breath, his mind clearly at work. "Which school do you think they'll hit?"

"Hard to say. Most of the fires have been strung between here and Riverton. Given their proximity to one another, these kids could be from either community. Possibly both."

Technically, The Sisters was comprised of two distinct towns, founded by the daughters of cotton baron Bertram Randolph. Naomi lay on the north side of the railroad track, Juliet to the south. The towns shared most community services, including their three-man police force, the volunteer fire department, and an independent school district. For brevity's sake, most people simply referred to the twin cities as The Sisters. Riverton, the county seat, was less than thirty miles away.

"That's not the worst of it," Cutter continued. "I'm afraid the fire is only part of their masterplan."

"What do you mean?"

"That last fire, the one on Old Tap Road. There were people inside. They all got out safely, but there are reports of kids watching—and laughing—from the nearby wood line."

The worry on Brash's face etched deeper. "You think they'll set fire to the school while it's in session."

Cutter's expression was solemn. "Folks think banning guns will solve the problem. But just like with meth labs and gray hairs, you can pull one weapon, but another always pops out."

Brash nodded. "Like Granny Bert always says, to pull any weed, you have to get down to the root."

# 9

Madison and Granny Bert returned to the inn and went straight to their room, more than a bit rattled. Madison didn't even fuss at her grandmother for creating such a scene. While she returned a missed call from Derron, she heard her grandmother calling the mall to apologize for her clumsiness. Although she offered to pay for damages, the owner assured her it wasn't necessary, especially when they heard about her upcoming operation.

"Granny!" Maddy hissed, just as Derron answered.

"Dollface, you'll be happy to know our ad is already paying off! We have two new clients."

"Did we get the maternity leave job? What kind of business is it?"

"We don't have that one yet. But we are filling in a sales position at a store in Brenham, after the owner broke her foot. That should be good for at least a month."

"What about the other job?"

"That's the one I'm calling about. I want to know how I should proceed with it."

"You'll have to tell me more about it."

"It's... rather delicate," her employee hedged.

"Derron. I don't like the sound of your voice. What

have you gotten us into?"

"It's a worthy cause, I swear. I'm just not sure what to do. It's a surveillance case, more or less."

Madison didn't bother holding back a groan. "Derron, you know I'm not a fan of surveillance." Her first surveillance case had concluded with his mother's death. "These never seem to end well."

"But this is a father, and he's desperate."

"Is his child missing? If so, call Brash."

"She's not missing, but he is afraid of losing her. He thinks she's mixed up with the wrong friends."

Madison's sigh was weary. "All parents worry about that, Derron. It's one of the requirements of our job."

"You don't understand. He's a single father and he's worried about his only child. He wants us to start immediately. He even paid the priority fee."

"What priority fee?"

"The one I invented for the ad. Pay the fee, and you jump to the front of our heavy case load."

"You mean in front of Miss Sybil's weekly pharmacy runs and walking Glitter Thompson's dogs," Madison broke in dryly. "*Heavy* only if we carry the dogs, rather than use the leashes."

"You know we aren't at liberty to discuss our other clients and the specifics of their needs." He sounded like a prim and proper rule follower, not the flamboyant color-outside-the-lines character Maddy knew him to be. "Our new customers are loving it. If they mention the ad, we offer a 25% discount."

"And it *worked*?"

"Two new clients so far, both priority," Derron beamed.

"So what's the problem, other than the fact there's only one of you, I'm fifteen hundred miles away, and we now have two priority cases?"

"I can handle the double booking, girlfriend. The

problem is that I'm a man. I can't very well follow a sixteen-year-old girl around, now can I?"

"Hmm. I see your point. Does she go to The Sisters High?"

"No, Riverton."

"Okay, let's do this. Ask the kids if they happen to know her. Get Bethani to look her up on social media and see if they have any mutual friends or interests. I'll be back by the weekend, so it's only a few more days. In the meantime, have the twins dig up as much as they can about this girl."

"Great. Sounds like a plan."

"Perfect. Call me if you have anything else pop up."

"Will do, dollface. Oh, any word on your luggage?"

"Don't even get me started," she warned. "I can't believe how cavalier the airport has been about this. It's not like my luggage wasn't clearly identifiable, inside and out. It's hard to believe someone just kept it, knowing they could return it to the right person."

"I've seen your wardrobe. Maybe they thought they were doing you a favor."

"Gee, thanks."

"Maybe now you'll let me take you shopping."

"Genny took me last night."

"Stay and shop all you like," he suggested. "Don't bother rushing home. I'm more than happy to keep your hunky boyfriends occupied while you two are gone."

Madison chuckled, as he knew she would. "I just bet you are. But remember. Hands off."

His sigh carried over the miles. "The good ones are always taken."


Still worked up over her missing luggage, Madison decided to look through the piece she had in the closet. Perhaps she had overlooked a clue.

Dragging the suitcase onto the bed, she removed its contents, piece by piece. Out of common courtesy and a respect for the other person's privacy, she had avoided rifling through it too thoroughly, but this was ridiculous. If the airport couldn't find a solution to her dilemma, she would find one herself.

She pulled out three folders, all stuffed with random papers. Granny Bert was right; most of this was gibberish. Some of the papers had row after row of computer-generated letters, sorted in neat order by the length sequence. Some rows had a string of only six letters; others stretched into two dozen or more characters. None formed coherent words. Other papers were handwritten, again in seemingly random words, letters, and even shapes. Had they not been written in such a neat hand, she would think it the work of a child. One of the folders contained nothing but numbers, sorted in chronological order by the length of the digit string, which again ranged from six to a dozen or more characters.

Madison shrugged and set the folders aside, still clueless as to their purpose.

Two books lay beneath the folders, and both were heavy. Living near communities back home with heavy Czech populations, Madison was familiar with some of their native language. She saw very few words she recognized, but enough to feel the book was Slavic in nature. Polish, perhaps? Bulgarian? Maybe even Russian, if those backward letters were any indication. The other book was filled with the symbol-like characters of the Japanese or Chinese language. It also portrayed several pages of colorful, if not simplistic, artwork.

Madison set the books aside, as well.

There were only a handful of other items in the

suitcase. A standard ledger book, filled with the usual notations and numbers. At last, something that made sense, although the figures were meaningless out of context. A small handheld device, with some sort of light bar attached to it. It reminded Madison of a mini version of the black light Blake had received for Christmas. A stack of construction paper, cut into squares and bound with a rubber band. Three fountain pens in expensive cases. A roll of mints.

Absolutely nothing memorable or obviously valuable. It almost looked like the forgotten dregs of someone's work locker.

*Perhaps that's it.* Someone had changed jobs or been fired. This was the last of their personal items, random as they seemed. No wonder they hadn't bothered to claim them. The ledger, however, might be important, but she couldn't worry about it. Perhaps the company folded and the books no longer mattered.

She searched the lining one last time, looking for some tucked-in piece of identification. All she uncovered was a narrow slip of paper, most likely one left by the manufacturer as part of quality control. *LILAC* most likely identified a particular inspector. The random numbers beneath it were factory related.

With a defeated sigh of resignation, she stuffed the items back into the luggage and stashed it in the closet. So much for that idea. All she could hope for was an honest individual on the other end. Hopefully, whoever had her luggage would do the right thing and return it to the airport, if not directly to her.

"Find anything?" her grandmother asked, returning from the other room.

"Nada."

"Maybe yours will still show up. It's only been one day."

"Maybe," she agreed, but she sounded skeptical. "I wonder how Genny's doing with her judging? Stuffing her face with all sorts of delicious desserts, I'll bet."

"She may not be hungry tonight."

"We'll drag her along, anyway. Like you said, this is not only a girl trip, it's her bachelorette trip."

Granny Bert pumped her hands above her head and wiggled her hips. "Par-tay."

"Granny, you crack me up!" Madison laughed, grabbing her grandmother and smothering her in a bear hug. "I'm glad you changed your mind and came along with us."

The older woman pretended to sputter and spout. "Someone had to show the bride-to-be a good time."

"If anyone can, it will be you." Madison released her grandmother and consulted her watch. "We have a couple of hours still before Genny gets back. What would you like to do?"

"I hear there's a jigsaw puzzle table down in the basement. You know I'm a master of the craft." Her eyes twinkled as she rubbed her wrinkled hands together.

"Then let's find this table and let you get to work. Can I just call the airport, one more time?"

"Go on with your calls. I'll be down in the basement when you're done."

"Are you sure?"

"I'll have my cell phone on me, and I'll ask that nice Percy to personally escort me down. I'll be good for a few hours, at least."

"Maybe I should go down with you..."

Granny Bert hoisted her hands onto her hips and gave her an evil eye. "Now you're just insulting me."

Madison backed off, her palms in the air. "Sorry. My mistake. Go enjoy yourself, and I'll be down shortly."

Her grandmother had one last remark before going out the door. "Don't go getting yourself into any trouble, you hear?"

"That's a bit like the pot calling the kettle black," Madison laughed, "but okay. Like you said, what could go wrong?"

# 10

Madison called the airport, patiently making her rounds through a half-dozen departments, but after an hour, the results were the same. Her luggage was nowhere to be found.

She took her time winding down to the basement, exploring along the way. Where better to start, she decided, than their own suite? The night before, she had been too upset about her suitcase to care, but her curiosity had finally kicked in.

In the adjacent area off the hallway, Madison found long, angular spaces and numerous nooks and crannies. She discovered a private deck and what she supposed was the fire escape. It looked more like a stylish exterior staircase, blending well into the architecture of the house turned hotel. Back inside, a steep and narrow set of steps led to the loft and Genny's would-be sleeping accommodations. Skylights kept the space light and airy.

Sophie said any unlocked door was fair game, so Madison helped herself. She found utility closets and attic access, a generous half bath and the sitting room with its wall of windows. Overhead was the most interesting feature of all: the cupola that towered above the very top of the mansion.

Madison peeked down from the windows, finding that the lower level actually offered a more panoramic and specific view than this smaller, higher height. The angle made it difficult to see well, but she thought she recognized the arm of a familiar black jacket, far below.

Suddenly uncomfortable in the rambling space, Madison left the room, firmly shutting the door behind her. She hurried down the narrow steps and crossed the suite to the more spy-friendly windows.

Madison bit her lip, regretting the choice of words rambling through her head. She wasn't spying. She was observing.

She parted the curtains, all the same.

There were only two people below. A maid swept up some shattered glass on the floor, while a guest stood aside, apologetic chagrin coloring her face. Either Mr. Black Jacket left the room, or she had been mistaken.

"Enough of this cloak and dagger stuff," Madison said aloud. She grabbed her sweater, tucked her key card in one pocket and her phone in the other, and headed out the door.

She descended to the library on the second floor, deciding to continue her exploration. The hallway across the library led to a handful of locked suites and another downward staircase. Madison followed the steps down to the West Wing, where a whole other world of suites appeared.

By the time she returned to the library to get her bearings, she agreed with Genny; this house was a maze! She wondered how long it took new employees to find their way around the intricate halls and intersections.

They should consider putting in traffic signs, she snickered to herself.

She looked up, into the partial open ceiling of the library, and saw something even better. Smoke signals.

Not literally, of course, but the chandelier on the third floor threw a random pattern of shadows onto the soaring ceilings, reminding Madison of smoke signals. The pattern of oddly shaped loops and swirls reminded her of something else, too, but she couldn't quite place it. Besides, she liked the idea of smoke signals better.

As she took to the stairs, she realized the museum hadn't covered smoke signals. There was a section dedicated to Native Americans—primarily the Navajo and Comanche so-called 'Code Talkers,' who sent vital messages past the enemy by using their native tongue—but nothing on smoke signals. She was surprised Granny Bert hadn't picked up on the oversight. She boasted of having Native American ancestors, but so far, genealogy records were a bit fuzzy on any direct bloodlines.

After her round-about path to the basement, Madison found her grandmother holding court with two men, engaged in a lively game of poker. All three chewed on unlit cigars and nursed glasses of whiskey and Coke.

"Ah, there she is now!" Granny Bert said, seeing her granddaughter descend the stairs. "Maddy, these fine gentlemen are fans of *Home Again*. Maury here wants your autograph."

"Oh, I don't really do autographs," she hedged. She had been burned on that front once before, when a restaurant patron asked her for her autograph and left Madison footing her bill.

"Please?" the man said, flashing his best smile. "It's for my daughter. She's a huge fan."

"I don't have any paper on me." She made a show

THE LILAC CODE

of patting her pockets, ignoring the telltale crinkle she heard in one.

"You could use that piece stuck to the bottom of your shoe," her grandmother scoffed dryly.

Embarrassed, Maddy swooped down to retrieve the unwanted tag-along and stuffed it in her pocket.

Maury watched with eyes that seemed to laugh at her. "Here. I just happen to have some right here." He dug in his pocket and pulled out a square of blue paper. The vibrant color wasn't a normal shade for notepads. He offered a sheepish smile along with a one-word explanation. "Grandkids."

"Do you have a pen?"

The other man produced a stylish pen, leaving her no excuse not to scrawl her name across the paper. "Shall I address it to anyone in particular?" she asked.

"Just your name is fine."

As Madison handed him the square with her name scribbled across the middle, Granny Bert cackled with glee. "See there! I'm all paid up!" She laid her cards down with a flourish, revealing a royal flush. "Read 'em and weep boys, read 'em and weep."

"Granny! You used my autograph as your ante?"

"Sure did." Her grandmother smirked, raking in the pile of cash on the table. "And to show my appreciation, I'll buy dinner tonight for you and Genny. Fellas, where do you suggest I take them?"

"I always eat at *Royal Taj* when I'm in the area," Maury said. "Great atmosphere, personal attention, and delicious Indian cuisine."

Her grandmother perked up. "Native Indian? My great granddaddy was a Cherokee Chief, you know."

"Not that kind of Indian food, Granny," Madison corrected her.

"Oh. Not sure I like any other kind."

"If you go, I suggest you try the Shrimp Tikka

Masala and garlic naan bread," Maury said.

Granny Bert tucked her winnings into her purse. "Well, fellas, I guess this is my cue to exit. Sorry to take your money and leave, but we've got a big evening ahead."

"Promise us a chance to win it back," the second man said. "Tomorrow afternoon, same place, same time?" He stabbed at his pocket with his pen, not bothering to see if he hit his target. When taking the pen from her hand, he automatically clicked the end to close it, not realizing Madison had already done so. She watched in amusement as the open tip now left fine markings along his pocket's rim.

Her eye snagged on the unusual color of the pen. Crafted in gleaming orange-stained wood, she knew she had recently seen a similar one. But where?

It nibbled on her mind, creating a vague sense of unease as she and her grandmother took the stairs to the first floor. "I wish I would quit doing this," she muttered in aggravation.

"You're the one who came down," Granny Bert shot back. "I told you, I was fine on my own."

"I'm not talking about the stairs. But seeing as you used my autograph to cover your bets, I'd say it's a good thing I showed up when I did."

The older woman conveniently ignored the truth. "Then what are you complaining about?"

"I keep seeing something and I think it reminds me of something else, but I can't ever quite put my finger on it."

"What do you keep seeing?"

"That's just it, it's always something different."

"Your mind is obviously distracted."

"I guess losing my luggage has me unsettled. I've never heard of anyone losing their carry-on luggage. That normally only happens to checked baggage."

"If something strange is going to happen, it's going to happen to you," Granny Bert acknowledged.

Maddy wrinkled her nose in protest, but found the claim impossible to refute. Her grandmother had a point.

"So what brings your poker buddies to Peralynna?" Madison asked.

"A business deal in the area. They say they like it here because of the oversized rooms."

"Ours is certainly huge, even without the loft."

"There's room enough up there for a party, you know," her grandmother said, slipping her a sly look. "I could make a call. Find us an entertainer for this evening. Something to make Genny's bachelorette party a little more memorable."

"No male stripper, Granny. I already told you that."

"What about a scantily dressed male dancer?"

"No."

Granny Bert turned her head away with a sniff. "I hope Brash realizes he's marrying an uptight fuddy-duddy."

"I heard that."

"So, what do you have planned?"

"I thought we'd go out for a nice dinner. Maybe a movie."

"You really know how to paint the town red, don't you?" her grandmother muttered. "A weak, sickly pink, at best."

"Fine. We'll let Genny decide. And look, there she comes right now." She waved to draw her friend's attention. "Uh-oh. She looks exhausted."

"It's hard work, standing around eating all day. The poor child. Think of all the crème brulee, crepes, and chocolate ganache she had to endure."

Madison elbowed her grandmother into

submission as Genny approached, her blond hair in disarray.

"Rough day, my friend?" she smiled sympathetically.

"Something like that. You know how difficult celebrities can be."

"You should've served it right back to them!" Granny Bert huffed. "You're a celebrity in your own right. Even before you opened your own restaurant in Naomi and starred on *Home Again*, you were a well-known pastry chef. That's why you're the one judging them. Don't let 'em try to one up you, girl."

"Thanks, Granny Bert," Genny said with a tired smile. Blood kin or not, Granny Bert always stood up for her, just as she did for the rest of her clan. Despite her mild insults and gruff ways, the older woman was a natural-born mama bear when it came to family.

"If you're too tired to go out tonight, Genny, we could have something delivered," Madison offered.

"Give me thirty minutes to unwind and freshen up, and I'm good. Just don't be offended when I decline dessert."

"You didn't happen to bring us back samples, did you?" Granny Bert asked hopefully.

"Better than that," Genny said, the twinkle reviving in her blue eyes. "Tomorrow, we're filming here at the hotel, so you can sample them fresh from the oven!"

# 11

"Here you go, Derron. My very first official report as an *In a Pinch* employee." The teenager dropped a neatly typed sheet of paper onto his desk, her blue eyes twinkling. Bethani often claimed to inherit her blond hair and blue eyes from her 'aunt' Genny, when in fact she owed that particular gene to her late father.

"Good job, girlfriend!" Derron looked over the information, clearly impressed with its thoroughness. "That was fast. You even included links, I see."

"We're now friends on her favorite social media sites, SnapChat and TeenMix."

"Never heard of that one."

"You're not a teen," she reminded him sweetly.

"You hurt me, girlfriend."

Bethani was unaffected by his pretty pout. "Ask me about your newest mark."

"She's not a *mark*. And where did you get this lingo, anyway?"

"PI 101." She grinned. "You're spying on this girl, aren't you?"

"I am not," Derron denied with righteous indignation. He tossed his stylish blond head and demurely added, "You're doing it for me."

Eager to show off her investigative skills, Bethani skipped the banter. "So, go ahead, ask me about her."

"Where does she hang out?"

"*DQ* parking lot, somewhere called Bookerman's Bridge, and TeenMix chat rooms."

"Favorite color?"

"Purple and black."

"Music?"

"Texas Music."

He looked up in surprise. "That's a thing?"

Bethani stared at him, dumbfounded. "Seriously? You call yourself a Texan and you don't know what Texas Music is?"

"I'm a blues kind of guy, myself."

"I suppose you've heard of Willie and Waylon, Steve Earl, Eli Young Band, Ben Morris and The Great American Boxcar Chorus, Aaron Watson, Lyle Lovett, just to name a few?"

"Yeah, yeah. Luckenbach and Gruene Hall. I get it." He waved it away with an air of disinterest. "Friends?"

Bethani squirmed as she twisted a lock of her long, blond hair. "That's the thing. I get the feeling this girl doesn't have very many friends. To tell you the truth, I feel kind of sorry for her."

"Home life?"

"Non-existent, according to her. Her dad's always at work. Mom died a couple of years ago." Tears pricked at her eyes. "I get it, you know? Losing your father is hard enough. I can't imagine what it must be like to lose your mom at that age."

His own eyes turned misty. "It's not easy at any age." Even though Derron had often referred to his own mother as the Dragon Lady, it didn't make her death any easier. He cleared his throat and continued drilling her, even though most of the information she provided was on the paper. "Boyfriend?"

"She wishes. She has her eye on a loser named

Frankie. No idea what she sees in him. Nappy hair, baggy jeans, scruffy little beard. Looks sort of like Shaggy on *Scooby Doo*, you know?"

Derron made a horrific face. "So not my type."

"Mine either, my friend," Bethani agreed.

Until recently, she went for the same sort of guys Derron did, only younger. Short hair, button-down shirts, polished shoes, and polished smiles. The preppy type, the kind found in her upscale Dallas neighborhood. Moving to The Sisters had been a bit of a culture shock for the then-fifteen-year-old. In the early days of their arrival, she made fun of the local boys, mistaking them for hicks, but it hadn't taken long to fall for their laidback charm and polite country manners. She now preferred faded jeans to pressed khakis, scuffed cowboys boots to polished loafers, and pearl snap shirts to button-downs. Her date to prom was none other than Drew Baines, the president of the Future Farmers of America. Bethani knew if her friends in Dallas saw her with Drew, they would call her crazy.

Her friends here, however, called her the luckiest girl at Sisters High.

"Good work, Bethani. I'll put this in the file and show your mom how helpful you can be."

"Do you think she'll hire me?" the teen asked, her voice filled with hope.

"You mean, like pay you a salary?"

"That was the plan."

He considered himself lucky when Maddy was able to pay *him*, but he wisely held his tongue. "I can't really speak for your mom, but I'll stand by my offer. Help me with this case, and I'll take you shopping for your prom dress. I know all the best designers and how to get a one of a kind dress at off the rack prices."

The teen's shoulders sagged. "But unless I get a job

and have money of my own to pitch in, the only rack my mom can afford will be at Target."

Which was exactly why Maddy wouldn't hire her own daughter, a fact Derron didn't point out. "You're forgetting that I am a master negotiator, and that people can seldom resist my charm." He struck a pretty pose and batted his blue eyes. "Leave this to me, girlfriend. I won't let you down."

"Good. Because I have an idea about how to meet Tasha."

"I'm listening."

She hesitated for only a moment. "I'll need to borrow your car."

# 12

Dinner at *Royal Taj* was not only delicious, but educational. The owner personally made recommendations on which dishes to order and how to best enjoy the cultural experience. By the time the final glass of wine was poured, Granny Bert had a new favorite cuisine.

"I bet this would be even better with a little of my homemade salsa on it. Throw in a pot of red beans and cornbread, and you'd have a real feast."

"This isn't a red beans and cornbread kind of meal, Granny."

"What's wrong with red beans and cornbread? Use a little fatback for seasoning, and it's hard to beat a good pot of pinto beans. This naan is good, but there's nothing like cornbread to go with beans. Many a night, that's all we had for supper."

Knowing the subject would soon turn to walking five miles to school each day—through the snow, no less—and doing chores before dawn, Madison gently turned the topic toward Genny's upcoming wedding.

Midway through the conversation, Madison had the uneasy sensation of being watched. She subtly turned her head, pretending to work a crick from her neck. She didn't see anyone, but the feeling persisted. She asked Genny about the flowers for the ceremony as she shifted in her seat and peered deeper into the restaurant. She didn't see anyone returning her gaze.

"Are you okay, girl?" Granny Bert finally asked. "You act like you have ants in your pants."

"I think I'll find the little girl's room."

"It's right around the corner," her grandmother supplied.

"I'll be right back."

She spotted him on the way back to the table. He sat in the far corner of the restaurant, at a small table near the front. *Ready to dash out the door, no doubt.* The man from the airplane looked no more relaxed now than he did then. His eyes met hers for the briefest of moments, before he looked hastily away. Not before she felt their heated intensity.

"You look pale," Genny noted when she returned to the table. "This spicy food hasn't upset your stomach, has it?"

"It's not that. Granny, remember yesterday when you thought someone was following us?"

"You mean when I said, 'don't look now,' so you craned your neck around like a nosy giraffe?"

Madison made a face. "So, here's your chance to show me how it's done. Don't look now, but I think our friend is following us again."

"Okay," she said slowly. "Where is he?" To her credit, the older woman didn't as much as cut her eyes.

"Small table against the front wall. Near the door."

"I know Genny doesn't want dessert," Granny Bert abruptly changed the subject, "but the owner said they had a fabulous rice pudding here. I think I'll have some."

For a moment, Madison thought her grandmother

had lost her mind. Here she was babbling about dessert, instead of worrying about the potential danger of a stalker. When Granny Bert tossed her hand into the air and looked around for their waiter, Madison understood.

"Yoo-hoo," her grandmother called.

Dozens of diners looked up from their meal, including the lone man at the table near the door. Shattering the quiet murmur of the upscale eatery, Granny Bert continued, "Yoo-hoo, maître d. Hello. Can we get some dessert over here?"

Madison wanted to sink beneath the white tablecloth, but her grandmother's antics worked, yet again.

"Yep, that's the guy," Granny Bert chirped to her companions. "Same bulb nose and beady eyes."

"That's why that description sounded so familiar," Madison realized. "I saw that man on the plane. He wasn't at all happy about the delay we caused."

"He doesn't look too happy right now, either," Genny said. She was the only one with a direct line of sight to his table. "Why would he be following you, though?"

"He was seated near the bin where the attendant put my bag," Madison recalled.

"So, do you think he's the one who took your suitcase, and you have his?"

A flash of hope soared within her chest. It crashed just as quickly. "Maybe. But why wouldn't he approach me, instead of just following us around? He deliberately avoided my eyes just now."

"And he's leaving," her friend reported.

"Leaving?"

"Yep. Didn't even wait for the ticket. Just threw a wad of bills onto the table and is walking out right now."

"I don't like this," Madison admitted. "Something doesn't make sense."

"Maybe he's embarrassed." Genny rolled her hands as she talked out a scenario. "He took the wrong luggage, now he's shy about approaching an attractive woman. He's afraid of looking foolish. He knows you have the suitcase with his dirty underwear, he—"

"You can stop right there. First of all, there isn't a shy bone in this man's body. He has that take-charge attitude about him. Second, there weren't any dirty underwear. In fact, there weren't any clothes at all, just a bunch of junk. It looked like the bottom of someone's work locker." She shared with them her theory of someone's last day on the job.

"That's it, then. He lost his job and he's in a fowl and antsy mood. Now he has to go home and tell his wife why he has some other woman's unmentionables and how he lost not only his job, but his personal effects."

Madison rolled the theory around in her head before promptly discarding it.

"Nah, I didn't believe it, either," Genny admitted. "But there has to be an explanation."

"There is," Granny Bert said in her matter of fact manner. "He was doctoring the books, and you have his second ledger. He didn't report it to lost baggage because it could get him in trouble."

She hated to admit it, but her grandmother had a point. "Actually, that makes sense."

"If he knows you found the ledger, it could put you in a dangerous spot," Genny reasoned. "So how do you approach him with a switch, without letting him know you saw it?"

"I could say I recognize him from the plane and act like I'm terribly embarrassed, but does he happen to have my bag? I have someone else's bag full of folders. I don't have to mention the ledger or the light or the—" she stopped mid-sentence as another realization hit her "—pens." She twisted toward her grandmother. "Granny Bert, how much do you know about your poker pals back at the hotel?"

She shrugged her bony shoulders. "Not much. They're from Chicago and are in town to close a business deal. Maury is a widower and lives across the street from his daughter, who was a big fan of *Home Again*. She's the one he wanted the autograph for. Barton is divorced and doesn't have any kids. I'm not sure if that's his first name or his last, but he sure knows how to deal cards. Back in the day, he was a dealer in Atlantic City. He has a tiny hint of an accent, too, but I can't quite place it... And he has a thing for that Jamaican music. You know, the kind that makes you want to get up and dance."

"Calypso music?" Genny guessed.

"Yeah, that's it. He kept on about it, asking me if I liked it and watching me real close to see my answer. Oh, and he's allergic to latex. The kind they use in personal protection."

Madison's mouth fell agape. "Really?" Sometimes, her grandmother was unbelievable. "How did you... oh, never mind. I don't even want to know. But did you happen to notice the pen he had in his pocket, the one he gave me to sign the autograph?"

"Yeah, he kept fiddling with it. It was one of his tells. Every time he bluffed, he'd click the top of it."

"Did you notice how it was a vibrant shade of orange? And quite expensive?"

"I didn't exactly see a price tag hanging from it like on old Minnie Pearl's hat, if that's what you mean."

"It was hand carved from wood, and the metal was gold plated. That translates to pricey."

"Which is why I buy those stick pens from the dollar store. When they run out of ink, you just toss them away."

Genny tried to speed the conversation along. "Why do you ask, Maddy?"

"Because I saw those same type of pens, or at least their wooden cases, inside that rolling bag. Both men having an expensive pen like that, in that color, can't be a coincident."

"Unless that's the company Maury and Barton are closing the deal with. Did you ever think of that?" her grandmother asked smartly.

"Actually, no. I didn't."

The waiter appeared at their table. "Your rice pudding, Madame."

"Could you wrap that up to go?" Granny Bert asked with a wave of her hand. "Guess my eyes were bigger than my stomach."

Maintaining his composure, the waiter forced a tight smile. "Certainly, Madame. As you wish."

Genny looked worried. "What if that guy is outside waiting on us? What do we say if he approaches us?"

"Don't worry," Granny Bert said. "I got this."

Maddy was almost afraid to ask. "What now?"

"Leave it to your old granny. I'll see that we get to our car safely. It'll be up to you to see that we get back to the hotel."

The waiter returned with her takeout bag and the bill. After leaving him a generous tip, Granny Bert led the way to the front, where she asked to speak to the owner. Despite having made quite the scene earlier, the sly older woman was nothing but charming as she profusely complimented the man for the fine meal and the wonderful introduction to his native cuisine. They chatted for several minutes and to Madison's surprise, it was the gentleman himself who suggested walking the ladies to their car.

Madison scanned the parking lot but didn't see their stalker. She wasn't taking any chances, however. After engaging the locks on the car, she deliberately turned in the opposite direction of their hotel. Genny's GPS could guide them with a different route to *Peralynna*.

"Granny, that was quite a performance back there," she said as she took a side street, her voice filled with a touch of awe. "I don't know how you do it."

"Finesse, my dear. Finesse." She patted her granddaughter's arm. "Don't worry, dear. Another thirty or so years, and you'll have it down, too."

"You do realize my grandfather was a saint, putting up with your shenanigans for over fifty years."

Granny Bert smiled at that. "Maybe Willie Nelson will write another song about me. He could call it The Angel and her Saint."

"I'm thinking more along the lines of The Swindler and the Saint."

"I'm thinking you should turn here," Genny broke in. "Because I think someone is following us."

# 13

They wound their way through the streets and neighborhoods, until they were certain no one followed. Then Maddy sped back to the hotel as fast as she could. They were now tucked safely inside their suite, where they discussed their options on how to proceed.

"Okay, girls, this is getting a little freaky." Genny was the first to admit the fact aloud.

Madison pulled the suitcase from the closet and set it in the middle of the floor. The three of them perched on the sofa and stared at the bag, as if expecting to find the answers within its generic black construction.

"We could take it to the police," Genny ventured.

Madison chewed on her lip. "But what good would that do? They won't know who the owner is, anymore more than we do."

"But it will get it off our hands."

Granny Bert snorted in disagreement. "Yeah, but Beady Eyes won't know that. He'll still follow us around, thinking we have his bag."

"You could call Brash and ask his opinion."

Maddy loved the man with all her heart, but he

was too protective of her. "Which would be to get on a plane and come home. End of story. You know how my fiancé is."

"Exactly like mine. So, we're in agreement? No need to worry the guys back home when we can handle this ourselves."

"Agreed."

Genny's dimple appeared. "What's that old handshake we used to have?" She put out a fist.

Madison topped it with her own and together they circled their free hands over their fists. "Girl Code!" they called in unison. "Always have your sister's back!"

They dropped their hands, laughing. "We haven't done that in years!"

"The last time I remember doing it was when we both agreed not to buy that silver dress for senior prom."

"I remember that," Granny Bert recalled. "That was one of the biggest squabbles you girls ever had. You both found that silver dress and fell in love with it. Trouble is, it made Genny look like a shiny elephant and Maddy like a candy wrapper. I was secretly glad you fought over it, so that neither one of you embarrassed yourself in it."

Their laughter slowly died away, leaving an empty echo in the room. Right alongside the mixed-up luggage.

Genny stood and circled the offending piece. She tapped her pursed lips as she thought aloud. "I suppose we could open it. One more time, just to see if you missed something."

"Maybe you'll see something I didn't."

Genny stood back, reluctant to move forward.

"Go ahead," Madison encouraged, her voice tight. "Open it."

Her friend recoiled, as if scorched by her tone. "I'm not going to open it. You open it."

When neither moved to do so, Granny Bert let out a loud huff. "Oh, for Heaven's sake! It's not like there's a bomb inside. I'll open the cotton pickin' thing!"

Maddy motioned her heroic gesture away. "I've got it," she said, falling to her knee and unzipping the case.

She pulled out the folders, handing the first to Genny, the next to Granny Bert, and keeping the final one for herself. All three women did a thorough perusal of the folder they held, before rotating them for a triple inspection.

"Gibberish," Granny Bert concluded, holding the folder with the illogical letters and drawings.

"Random strings of numbers," Genny said, flapping her folder.

"Names of people and places, but not necessarily addresses."

They passed a helpless look among themselves, having no clue what any of it meant.

"There's two books, neither written in English." Madison handed one to each woman. "I only know limited Latin and Spanish, and these are neither."

"It almost looks like Czech or Polish, but I think it's more likely Russian," Granny Bert said, thumbing through her book.

"Is this Chinese?" Genny wondered aloud. She fingered the illustrations in the back. "Cute artwork. I saw this one with all the loopty-doops drawn in the folder with the handwritten notes. It almost looks like a child's drawings, yet it doesn't. Too deliberate, even if it is dreadfully simple."

"That was my take," Madison agreed. "Granny?"

She and Genny exchanged books. "These aren't conventional books," she noted. "No ISBN, no imprint. They weren't intended for the public."

"This gets weirder and weirder. Do you think they may be some sort of office manual?"

"I guess they could be," Genny said, but her tone was doubtful. She tested the weight of the one she held. "This one would make a good doorstop. Or a club."

Digging back inside the bag, Madison continued. "Next, we have the ledger. It looks standard enough. No identifying business headers, but the usual notations as far as dates, expenditures, that sort of thing. Maybe you'll see something I didn't."

Genny carried the ledger to the sofa and sank down into the cushions to study its pages.

"Is that a black light?" Granny Bert asked. "Your father used to have one of those, back in his disco days. Dad-blamed thing always hurt my eyes," she complained. "Turned everything fuzzy."

Madison turned the light strip over in her hands. "They have something like this that detects fingerprints. It's a lot less messy than dusting for prints, but much more expensive. Obviously, The Sisters Police Department doesn't have one."

"So, there's Brash's souvenir, right there in your hand," Granny Bert said with a smart nod.

"I can't just take this."

"Why not? No one's claiming it."

Madison shook her head, slightly exasperated with her grandmother. Anyone who didn't know the woman might take her seriously. As she often did, Madison simply ignored her. "Then we have blocks of paper, a roll of mints, and these pens. See? The cases match the pen your poker buddy had."

"Do they all have pens inside?"

"I don't know. We'll see." She opened one for confirmation, rattling the other two for sound. "Yes.

Appears brand new and never used."

Genny looked up from the ledger. "Is there anything special about the bundle of note paper?"

Madison turned the bound bundle over in her hands, noting the colorful array of options. She had originally mistaken the squares as construction paper, but upon closer inspection, she realized they were made of a much finer quality paper. "Not really." She shrugged. "They look like Post-It notes, without the sticky strip. Only the paper has more texture to it and the colors are much more vibrant. Oh, wait. There is something special about it," she corrected, her voice quickening. "Maybe not special, but familiar. Granny, doesn't this look like that piece of paper your friend had? The one I wrote my autograph on?"

"Looks like the same shade of blue."

Madison rubbed it between her fingers. "It feels the same, too. I remember I had a bit of trouble, getting the pen to write at first."

"Okay, so I'm confused," Genny said. She put her hands on either side of her head. "Do we think this case belongs to Beady Eyes, or to your poker buddies? Beady Eyes was on the plane and is following you around town, but your poker buddies have items that match the ones in the bag."

Madison bit her lip. "I know. I'm not sure which one of them it belongs to."

"Maybe all three work for the same company," Granny Bert suggested. "Beady Eyes flew in from Houston to help them close the deal."

They tossed around several more suggestions, without any clear conclusions.

"Let me meet with the guys for another round of poker tomorrow afternoon. I'll ask a few more questions about their business and why they're in town," Granny Bert said. "Maybe I can work the conversation around to lost luggage."

"I'm coming with you," Madison insisted. "I don't want you alone with them in that basement."

"Remember," Genny said, "we're filming a segment of the show here tomorrow morning, if you want to watch."

"Sounds fun." Madison put items back into the bag. "Are you seeing anything in that ledger?"

"Just standard stuff. There's no way to know whether these are doctored figures, or not. I don't even know what company they belong to." She shrugged and handed the book back to her friend. "Can I see one of those pens?"

"Sure." As Madison tossed a wooden case to her friend, something else floated through the air. "What was that?"

Genny picked up the tiny strip of plastic. "It looks like one of those little clear strips they put with batteries, to keep them deactivated until you need them."

Curious, Madison opened the other two cases. Upon closer inspection, she saw the same clear strip inserted into the ends of the pens. "That's odd. Why does a mechanical pen need a battery?" She fingered the finely carved instrument. "It's not like there's a digital calendar built in, or even a clock."

Genny's voice dropped to a whisper. "Maybe there's a mic inside."

Madison gasped and dropped the pen, box and all, as if it suddenly scorched her skin. "Why would these men need pens with hidden mics?"

"Unscrupulous business practices?" Genny suggested. "Spying on their competition?"

At the mention of spies, all three women fell quiet. Their eyes widened.

With a nervous gulp, Madison hastily stuffed the

items back into the bag. Granny Bert helped zip it, while Genny got up to pace the room.

Stashing the suitcase out of sight and, hopefully, out of mind, Madison turned and noticed her friend's antsy gait. "I guess this hasn't been a very fun girl trip, has it?" Her tone was rueful. "Instead of the male strippers Granny Bert suggested, we end up with a mystery on our hands."

"Hey, I like mysteries as well as anyone," Genny said, but the claim was weak. "I can do without the danger, but the mystery part is always fun. I guess this was the premonition I had."

"Just the same, I think I'd feel better if we all slept down here again tonight. I'll take my turn on the couch."

"Not on your life! I love sleeping on this thing. It's very comfy."

Settling in on the soft cushions, Genny tucked her feet beneath her and patted the empty space beside her. "Okay, enough of this cloak and dagger stuff," she proclaimed. "Grab a seat, girls. This is my bachelorette party, and I have an activity for us."

Granny Bert brightened. "We're going to call Chippendales, after all?"

"Not that. But we are going to have a nice, long girl talk."

She waited for both to be seated before giving Granny Bert the nod. "Granny Bert, you start. I'm getting married in a few days, and you have the most experience on the subject. What's your number one piece of advice for a happy marriage?"

After fifty-three years of a solid and happy marriage, the older woman's answer came without hesitation. "That's easy. Always be faithful. In body, mind, and spirit. No exceptions."

"I agree," Madison said, even though her late

husband didn't share the same philosophy.

"So do I." Genny nodded vigorously. "And that won't be a problem. I can't imagine wanting any man other than Cutter. He's my whole world."

"I don't carry on about it often," Granny Bert continued, "not like some folks do, shoving their beliefs down your throat whether you want it or not, but remember it takes three people to make a marriage work." She ticked them off on bony fingers. "Husband, wife, and God. The couple that prays together stays together. It's important to attend church together."

"It's important to attend everything together," Madison offered. "I know people who spend their holidays apart, because the wife goes to her side of the family, while the husband goes to his side. If you can't manage both, take turns."

"That's easy for us. You two are my family. And Cutter adores you, as much as I adore all the Montgomery clan."

"I know Cutter has been raised with the same values, the same sense of family. As long as you live your life as a couple, it won't ever be a problem," Madison said with confidence.

"Remember to give in once in a while," Granny Bert offered. "It's fun to win every argument and be right all the time but being on the losing end can start to wear on any man's pride. Know which battles to fight, and which ones to throw."

"I can't imagine you willingly throwing in the towel," Madison admitted to her grandmother.

"More times than you can imagine, child. You remember that old avocado green refrigerator we used to have?"

"The one that's still in the shed? The avocado wonder, as you call her?"

"That's the one. The ugly, bulkiest thing I ever did see, next to Dolly Mac Crowder. But your grandfather was bound and determined to buy it. He coveted its extra big freezer, knowing exactly how many cartons of Blue Bell ice cream he could fit in next to the fancy ice maker. I wanted the harvest gold in another brand, but I knew how important it was to him, so I finally gave in. It turned out to be one of the best purchases we ever made. The thing's been running like a charm since 1972." She gave a smart nod of her gray head and continued.

"And don't think I was in favor of letting your daddy go all wild like he did. I wanted him to stay in college and get a degree, but Joe thought we should give him room to spread his wings. Took a while, but the boy finally came in for a safe landing."

That 'boy' was almost sixty years old and, if the truth be known, he was still a bit wild. His life as a missionary allowed him to sow his oats, at least doing more good in the world than he did harm.

"Marriage is all about give and take," she continued. "A man can't go through life, barking out orders to his wife and expecting his wife's respect. A woman can't waltz around, making everything about herself and never giving any thought to what her husband wants. There has to be give and take. Give respect, you get respect. Give love and encouragement, you get love and encouragement."

"Always kiss the other one goodbye. Always say I love you," Madison advised. "You can't be sure it won't be your last opportunity." Even though she no longer loved her deceased husband, she wished she had said a proper goodbye. Like so many other times before that, they had parted on anger. It was one of her biggest regrets.

"Remember to laugh. Life is serious enough.

Lighten up every chance you get."

Madison agreed with her grandmother. "I know this won't be a problem with Cutter, but sit under the stars. Spend some quiet time there, just the two of you."

"Better yet, do the deed under the stars," Granny Bert advised, her wrinkled face softened with a long-ago memory. "There's nothing like it."

"Granny Bert! I can't believe you said that!" Both younger women spoke at the same time.

"Why not? We're all adults here. And at least once, you should give skinny dipping a try. But I do advise keeping your head about you and remembering where you are. One of the times when your grandpa tried it, he forgot it was time for the neighbor to make his evening drive around the pasture. The stock pond was near the fence line. Let's just say old man Cleaver got an eyeful." Her cackle of glee turned to a snort of jealousy. "And so did that wife of his! Don't think I didn't notice how she eyed your grandfather after that, like a butcher eying a side of prime beef. Poor old Cleaver always was a short, stocky man." She shook her head in pity for the other woman.

"Granny! The things you say!"

"I told you, girl, your grandfather was like my own gift from God. In more ways than one, if you know what I mean."

Madison and Genny broke down in peals of laughter. The mood of the evening lightened as Granny Bert entertained them with tales from fifty-three years of marriage. Long into the night, they swapped silly stories and remembrances, spiked with plenty of laughter and love.

When they finally crawled into bed in the wee hours of the morning, Madison couldn't help but gloat. "See, Granny? You can have a perfectly good bachelorette party, even without male strippers."

"I reckon," she allowed. "But a couple of dancers to remind me of your grandpa's finer features sure would have been nice."

# 14

"Come on, slowpoke. Aren't you ready yet?" Bethani asked her brother.

Blake slapped a Houston Astros World Champion hat on his blond head and opened the door. "You know this may get us grounded for life."

"I asked Mr. de if we could go," his twin replied defensively.

"But did you tell him why?"

"Sort of. I told him we were running an errand for Derron. And we are. Kind of."

"That's what I like about you, twin. Your directness."

"Shut your face and get in the car."

"Who said you could drive?"

"I'm the one who asked Derron if we could borrow his car, so obviously, I'm the one who gets to drive."

Blake grunted, but folded his long body into the passenger seat of the sporty little convertible. He paused in the act of buckling his seatbelt. "What is that black goop all over your face?"

"It's called eyeshadow."

"It's called Vampirina."

Instead of being insulted, his sister looked pleased. "Thanks. That's the look I was going for."

"You gotta be kidding me. You did that on purpose?"

"Didn't you do your homework on this case? Tasha is

into this look. If I want to make friends with her, I can't show up looking like a Susie Cheerleader."

"But you *are* Susie Cheerleader."

"She doesn't have to know that."

"You friended her on TeenMix. She'll know."

"I created a new account. My profile picture is a meme with a skull and roses."

"Don't think it'll work, but whatever." He glanced into the tiny backseat, noting it was vacant. "Where's Megan? You know she'll be pissed we're doing this without her."

"She had to help her mom with something. Besides, I'm not sure Megan could pull this off. She's too naturally perky."

"And you're not?"

Bethani pulled her face into a sullen scowl. It was a look she often wore in the days and months after their father passed away. Upon occasion, particularly around holidays and birthdays, the haunted look crept back into her face, hinting at the pain that still plagued her.

"Okay, so you know where the girl is coming from," Blake admitted. "But you've learned to live with the pain. Apparently, she hasn't."

"So maybe we can help her, did you ever think of that? We, of all people, know what it's like to lose a parent."

"Is that what this is all about? We're out to save this girl? I thought we were just narcing on her."

Bethani wiggled uncomfortably in her seat, as if the soft leather chapped her skin. "Maybe we could do both," she mumbled. It made her feel less guilty this way, imagining she could help the other teen.

"How do we even know she'll be there?"

"She hangs out every evening in the parking lot. She and those loser friends of hers."

"What makes you think they'll even talk to us?"

"I kind of set it up already. Here. Trade the cap for this hoodie."

"You gotta be kidding me!"

"Nope. Hold the wheel while I put mine on." With her brother's assistance, she stuffed the ends of her long, blond hair beneath a dark-purple knit cap.

"You look like it's a lot colder than fifty degrees out." The temps were already trending upward.

"Practicing for the ski trip."

He grunted and pulled a brown hoodie onto his own blond head. "I wore my best cap for nothing," he grumbled. "It was autographed, too."

"And you have on your good shoes," his sister criticized.

"Yeah, so? They matched the cap."

"You should have worn something scruffier. I'm guessing these kids aren't into baseball."

"It's America's past time!" Her brother was clearly offended.

"Maybe." A sliver of concern slipped into Bethani's voice. "But I don't think these are America's kids."


Two hours later, they were cutting their curfew woefully close.

"You sure you gotta go?" A dark-haired boy leaned onto the car window, leering down at Bethani as she slipped behind the wheel.

"It's our brother's car," she lied, "and we sort of borrowed it without asking. Gotta slip it back in the garage before he gets up. He works the late shift this week."

"Where's he work?"

"I dunno. Some lame job in Navasota or somewhere." She shrugged as if it made no matter to her. She pulled the door shut, barely giving him time to move back.

"Hey, I didn't get your number!" he called through the glass.

"Ask Tasha for it. We gotta blow."

She didn't give Blake time to fasten his seatbelt. She peeled out of the parking lot with the tires squealing, her foot heavy on the gas.

"Gag me!" Bethani said, spitting out her distaste for the boy. "What a total creep."

"Tell me about it. All he did was talk about blowing things up and burning things down, and some big bonfire they're having. He invited us to come."

"I know. So did that other creep, Julio."

"I noticed you were quite a hit with all the guys." It wasn't a compliment.

"Fresh meat," his sister acknowledged. "I have no idea what Tasha sees in those losers."

"I know. She actually seemed pretty cool."

Bethani slid her twin a keen look. "It looked like she thought you were pretty cool, too."

To her surprise, a flush of red crept up his neck. "You *like* her!" she cried in astonishment.

The normally confident teenager tried to sound indifferent. "She seemed cool. And she'd probably be pretty, if she'd take that black stuff off her face. I wasn't too crazy about the purple hair, either."

"I saw an old picture of her, before she went dark. You're right. She was really pretty."

"I was afraid they were going to recognize us from the show. That one girl kept going on and on about how familiar I looked."

"I think that was her way of flirting. She kept smacking her gum when she said it. I think to her, that was the equivalent of twirling her hair."

"She was just weird," Blake said with a frown.

"I don't think we have to worry about them recognizing us. None of them are the type to watch HOME TV. The BOMB channel maybe, but not HOME TV."

"You know that one guy is gonna call you."

Right on cue, Bethani's phone binged with a text. Blake

did the honors and read it off to her.

*See you Friday at the bridge? Freddy*

"Freddy Krueger," his sister muttered. "Where is this bridge, anyway?"

"Bookerman's Bridge, somewhere down a dirt road between here and home. I heard the guys talking about it. That's where the bonfire is, apparently. Out near an abandoned warehouse."

"What kind of warehouse is on a dirt road?"

"Oilfield, maybe?"

"Probably. There's a lot of those pumper things around here, like out on the deCordova Ranch."

"Speaking of deCordova, we need to tell Mr. de we're running late."

"Let's wait until we get back into Juliet. Maybe we can blame it on Derron. We have to take the car back, and we can say something about him yammering on and on about something."

"Which will probably happen."

"Exactly," his sister beamed. "So why not use it to our advantage?"

# 15

"Bethani? Blake?" Brash called from the kitchen, hearing the tattletale *bing* installed on all the doors at the Big House. "Is that y'all?"

"Yes, sir."

"I'm in the kitchen."

The duo tromped into the large eat-in kitchen, hoodies stashed out of sight. Bethani's dark makeup came off on the way home.

"Hungry? I saved you some leftovers, even though you said you'd eaten." With his hands in sudsy water, he could only nod toward the refrigerator. The kitchen was equipped with state-of-the-art appliances, all compliments from the sponsors of *Home Again*.

"I could go for something," Blake acknowledged, going straight to the over-sized built in. "I didn't have much at the *DQ*."

"You had a Triple-Buster, an order of fries, a shake, and a large Blizzard!" his sister protested. "I know, because I was paying!"

Her twin shrugged. "Like I said, I didn't have much. You want some of this?" He held the plastic container her way.

"I didn't even finish my own burger. Oh, yeah,

that's right. You ate the rest of mine, too."

Blake didn't bother heating the still-warm dish. "Not bad, Mr. de," he said. "What is it? Lasagna?"

"Spaghetti."

Blake considered the dish in his hands. "I could see that," he said thoughtfully. "Lumpy noodles, but not bad."

"A man should always know how to cook," Brash advised the teenager. "Remember that."

"Sorry we were a little late." Bethani breezed her way to the cabinet and retrieved a glass. "You know Derron. Yack, yack, yack." She did the thing with her hands, illustrating her point.

The man put down the dishtowel and leaned against the counter, crossing his long legs in front of him. "I know you were late getting to his house, too."

"Told you," Blake shot at his sister, stuffing the last bite of spaghetti into his mouth. "The man is a professional."

"I was afraid of driving too fast," Bethani explained. "I was in an unfamiliar car, you know. A girl can't be too safe."

"Come on, Beth. You can do better than that," Brash drawled.

"What do you mean?" she asked, her blue eyes wide and innocent.

"Can't you be a little more creative than that? You know, like it started to rain, and you couldn't find the control for the windshield wipers. Or you got detained by a herd of wild hogs crossing the road. Or you stopped to help someone change a flat tire. All, by the way, are in your best friend's little bag of tricks. Those are some of Megan's favorite excuses."

"Come to think of it, the fog was mighty thick," Blake joked.

"I don't do flat tires," Bethani sniffed, as if the very

thought was beneath her.

"In that case, I'll give you your first lesson, tomorrow after school."

Her blond head whipped around from the water spigot where she filled her glass. "Huh?"

"Just like a man should know how to cook, a woman should know how to change a flat tire. I'll be happy to teach you."

"Gee, thanks."

"No problem." He flashed a saucy grin before turning serious. "There's something I want to ask you two about. You were over in Riverton tonight, weren't you?"

"Yes," Bethani said slowly, wondering what else he knew. She added the respectful, "sir," as an afterthought.

"You know many kids over there?"

Blake was the one to answer. "A few. We met a couple more tonight."

"I hear a lot of the kids hang out in the *DQ* parking lot."

"It may be the county seat, but Riverton isn't much bigger than Naomi or Juliet put together. That's about all there is to do."

"I also hear there's some kids over that way that have an affinity for starting fires. You happen to hear anything about that tonight?"

"Man, he's good!" Blake said, clearly in awe.

Bethani jabbed her brother in the ribs and gave him a dirty look. "Real bright, Ajax," she muttered beneath her breath. She pushed back her hair and looked her soon-to-be stepfather more or less in the eye. "Why do you ask?"

His shrug was deceptively casual. "Just curious. I wouldn't want you mixed up with that kind of crowd, of course, but I was hoping you might have heard something. Cutter mentioned it to me today, so I just wondered."

"You're right, that's not the kind of crowd we usually hang with. We did meet a pretty cool girl tonight, though." She slid her brother a sly smile. "Didn't we, Blake?"

Her twin struggled to remain nonchalant, but a faint stain again crept into his cheeks. "She was okay."

"Oh? What was her name?" Brash cut the boy some slack, deliberately turning his back on him to save him further embarrassment.

"Tasha Garrison. Her dad works for the county, I think. Works in road maintenance or something."

Brash nodded. "Sure, I know him. He used to be a Road Commissioner for Precinct 1. He stepped down when his wife died a couple of years ago. Still works for the department, but said it was too much responsibility for a single father. He seems like a good guy."

Whether it was a fair practice or not, in all small southern towns, people were judged by their families. Brash knew Royce Garrison to be a fair and honest man, so he had no real objections to a potential friendship between the teens and the other man's daughter.

"She wanted us to come back and hang out Friday night," Bethani ventured to say, not at all certain she really wanted to go.

Instead of shutting her down like she suspected he might do, Brash seemed open to the possibility. "You'd have to ask your mother."

"Don't worry, I'd go along, too," Blake was quick to add. "Maybe Megan could come with us."

"Ask your mom first, and we'll see."

Bethani's phone binged. "This is Tasha now," she said, glancing down at the screen. "I think I'll go on up and get ready for bed. Night, Mr. de." She gave him a one-armed hug on her way out of the kitchen.

"Night, Beth. Megan's spending the night at her mom's, by the way."

In a way, it was a relief, knowing she didn't have to face her best friend. Megan would want all the details, and Bethani still hadn't sorted them out in her head. She thought she could become friends with Tasha.

It was the other kids that worried her.

# 16

The next day, simply seeing the cameras, crews, and lighting equipment needed for the cooking competition gave Madison horrific flashbacks to her own time behind the spotlight. *Never again*, she vowed for the hundredth time.

Genny scored her friends a table near the front of the action, to ensure a good line of sight and the best chance for samples. Granny Bert loved the attention, particularly when the celebrity chefs chatted with them during breaks. Madison enjoyed seeing her best friend in her element, not to mention learning a tip or two on baking. Taste testing the magnificent creations was a bonus.

Although the actual competition was filmed live, some of the promotional spots and segments not affecting the outcome of the contest were taped. For those, re-takes were often required. Dirty dishes in the background, a flubbed line, or a poorly displayed sponsor's product meant re-shooting the scene. During those tedious times, Madison doodled on her notepad. No cell phones were allowed in the great room during the competition.

She found herself drawing random designs, most of them simple scrolls and loops. Lazy art, Blake called it, because most of the designs flowed into creation without lifting the pen. It was the same concept behind writing in cursive, which led her to make a series of lower case l's, g's, p's and q's.

*The fun ones with loops*, she thought, scribbling lazily along. Granny Bert shot her a curious look, but Madison ignored her as she turned a g into the petal of a loosely formed flower. In fact, she discovered with amusement, if she adjusted the positions, she could turn four simple letters into a misshaped flower; g, l, an undotted j, and a p flowed together quite nicely to form the loops for petals. What was it Genny had called these last night? Loopty-doops?

Only then did her pen stutter. Madison did a double take, looking at the simple flower she had just drawn. She had seen this pattern before. Hadn't it been in the book, the one written in what they thought was Chinese?

Maybe, she decided, it was a psychology book, studying the hidden messages behind doodling. What did her doodling say about her? That she expressed herself through art? That she remembered proper penmanship? She heard that many elementary schools no longer taught cursive, as it wasn't 'computer-friendly.' Or did her doodling suggest that she was too lazy to lift her pen?

Thoughts of pens brought her mind back to her grandmother's poker buddies and the unique orange pens. Hidden mics or not, why did the same type pen appear in Barton's pocket and the mistaken bag? When it came to investigation, Brash had taught her not to believe in coincidences.

A private investigator based in Houston sometimes hired *In a Pinch* to do the menial grunt work when his cases ventured into Brazos Valley territory. It didn't seem that much different from some of her other cases, when clients hired her to provide surveillance or gather information used in settling minor disagreements, divorce cases, and the like. It was the *un*glamorous side of private investigation, but it paid the bills. She could charge more as a certified detective, so Madison was tossing around the idea of getting her own license. Brash was helping hone her investigation skills. Even if she never pursued her license, it was a useful talent to have, particularly as the mother of teenagers.

She thought about some of the lessons learned so far, rifling through tidbits of advice Brash offered during their tutoring sessions.

*Always question coincidence. Take nothing for granted.*

*Follow the money.*

*Greed is the root of all evil. Lust is a form of greed.*

*Go back to the beginning.*

*Pull a thread and see what it sews together.*

*God, I love it when you do that.*

Madison's face flushed with color as memories of their last 'tutoring session' flooded through her. Oh, the things that man had taught her about kissing! More often than not, they got sidetracked during her private lessons. Sometimes those sessions became a bit intense, as it had the night before she left.

As the parents of teenagers, they both agreed it was their responsibility to establish a strict moral code and to lead by example. If they couldn't abstain from sex, how could they expect it of their hormone-ravaged teens? *But good grief! If we don't get married soon, we're both going to spontaneously combust!*

Brash wanted to marry immediately, but Madison was determined not to steal the spotlight from her best friend. Even though she and Brash planned a small ceremony out at the ranch, she didn't want any part of this, her second wedding, to infringe upon her best friend's first wedding. After all the misery dear Genny had gone through—including an annulled twelve-hour justice of the peace marriage just out of high school and the path of destruction that followed—she deserved a special day of her own. Madison wanted to give that to her friend, even if it meant putting her own happily ever after on hold.

Gathering her thoughts back together like spilled secrets, Madison glanced around. Had anyone witnessed the drift of her mind? Seen the resulting flame in her cheeks? She let out a relieved breath. No one seemed to pay her any mind, including Granny Bert, who was busy making googly eyes at the chef in the competition. Her grandmother had several of his cookbooks, and now she had not only the man's autograph, but his cell phone number. Madison shook her head in wonder. *The woman can charm diamonds off a rattlesnake!*

Thoughts of her fiancé had gotten her so flustered she couldn't keep a coherent thought in her head. Where was she? Oh, yes, threads of evidence. So how did loopty-doop flowers, pens with secret recording devices, colorful notepaper, and Beady Eyes tie together? The man hardly seemed the type to appreciate artistic creations, particularly those that looked so childish.

Childish art.

The memory of the little girl at the airport flitted through Madison's mind. The child had handed her a picture of a crudely drawn flower, much like the one Maddy had just doodled on the paper. A picture drawn on a colorful square of paper.

Had she kept the picture, or had she tossed it away? Madison frantically tried to recall what had become of the note. She remembered stuffing it into her pocket.

She patted at her pockets now, feeling nothing. She still wore the same sweater. The sweater that had crinkled with the sound of paper, only yesterday. The sweater whose pockets were now empty, save for her room key. She must have dropped the note, or inadvertently thrown it away.

"I'm going to run up to the room," she whispered to her grandmother as she slipped silently from her chair. With any luck, housekeeping hadn't cleaned their room yet and she might find it there, crumpled on the floor or in the trashcan.

Madison slipped from the room, ignoring glares from the television team. For the sake of discretion, she used the front staircase, furthest from the filming. As she crossed the catwalk overlooking the great room, trying not to make any noise that would carry down below, she noticed movement out on the back deck. From here, she had an excellent view of the man making his way around the side of the hotel, wearing a familiar black jacket. His face was familiar, too.

Beady Eyes.

That meant he was here at the hotel. The man from the airport—the one who followed them from the museum to the old cotton mill, the one who watched her at the restaurant yet avoided meeting her eyes, the same man who most likely had taken the wrong suitcase by mistake—was definitely here at *Peralynna*.

*Always question coincidence.*

Madison hurried down the hall and into the library. As she started up the final staircase, she glanced up, praying that Beady Eyes/Black Jacket hadn't somehow beaten her to the third floor. Once again, her eyes were drawn to the shadows thrown onto the ceiling by the chandelier. Was it her imagination, or did those loops mimic the loops of her doodling, the same ones repeated in the book, and in the note?

"Come on, Maddy," she chided herself aloud, "you're letting your imagination run wild. Those are shadows, not smoke signals. Not secret spy codes. This isn't a spy house, and no one's chasing you. There has to be a perfectly good explanation for what's going on."

She let herself into the suite and rushed to the wall of windows, desperate to prove herself wrong. From here, she could see not only the great room, but through each of its windows.

"See?" she smirked. "Beady Eyes/Black Jacket isn't even out there. The deck is empty."

She allowed her eyes to make their way upward, to the corner window that offered a bird's eye view of the second-floor balcony. She saw a man disappear from sight. He was only visible from the waist down, but there was no denying he wore a black jacket.

"He's on his way up," she realized.

Her phone binged with a message. Per studio demands, she left her cell phone here in the suite while watching the competition. She retrieved it from the fireplace mantel and saw three missed calls, all from an unknown number.

Tension moved into her chest.

The phone vibrated as a message came through, startling her so badly that she dropped the phone. Scooping it up, she saw the one-word message.

***Trade?***

A picture of her suitcase followed. She knew it was hers, because the arm of her gown hung limply from one side. Something about the staged photograph was distinctly threatening, bringing to mind a headless body. Madison gulped.

She jumped again, as she heard the handle rattle on the suite's front door. She held her breath, waiting for housekeeping to identify themselves. No one called out, merely another rattle of the handle. As quietly as she could, Madison tiptoed toward the door and sidled up to the peephole. She bit back a gasp when she recognized Barton, Granny Bert's poker buddy. He jiggled the handle again.

Madison watched in amazement as he stepped back, lowered a beefy shoulder, and rushed forward. She jerked back just in time, feeling the air quiver with reverberation. The door moved but held.

Madison grabbed the nearest thing she could find, a narrow sideboard that looked antique. It was heavy, but she gave it a mighty shove, sliding it in front of the double doors. She kept it an inch or so away, hoping not to give away her presence in the room.

She had to think. If Barton was at the front door, and Black Jacket came up the fire escape to the back entrance, they had her trapped. Her only choice was to go up. She stuffed her phone in her pocket, thinking she could call for help along the way.

Something colorful caught her eye as she headed for the hallway. It was the note from the little girl, crumpled on the floor near the fireplace. It must have fallen from her sweater when she pulled her phone from her pocket. Maddy swooped down to retrieve it as she eased open the side door, afraid Black Jacket had somehow gotten in from the back deck.

The coast was clear. He had to wind his way across the different decks, zigzagging up the stylish fire escapes, before making it to the third floor. It bought her some time. She darted into the hall leading to the back exit. The deck chairs were stored indoors for the winter, so she wedged one of them beneath the door handle before scampering up the narrow staircase to the attic bedroom.

She paused by the windows at the top of the landing. She had a good view of two levels of decking. It would be a long fall, but she could jump to the second-floor deck, directly below her. But she still didn't see Black Jacket, which meant he was most likely between the two levels. She would fall directly into his path.

She nixed the idea and moved forward, further into the loft. Her phone binged as she entered the fourth level sitting area.

*I'm losing patience.*

Madison moved to the windows, peering down to the great room below. Filming was still in progress. She could still see the mirror above the staircase, and the reflection of a man's legs as he stepped off the bottom step. Moving on to scan the decks outside, she didn't see Black Jacket or Barton, meaning they were probably still on the third level, trying to enter the suite. Would she hear them if they did?

Just as she wondered where Maury was during all this, she glanced back at her grandmother and saw the answer. Granny Bert smiled up at her poker buddy as he took the seat she had recently vacated. At this distance, she couldn't be sure, but she thought he tilted his head up, probably scanning the wall of windows below her, wondering if his friends made it into the suite. Maddy ducked away, afraid he might see her, one tier up.

She dialed her grandmother's phone, belatedly remembering phones were prohibited during filming. By now, panic had addled her brain. She never thought to pull up the hotel's website, locate their number, and call for help. All she could think of was that she *couldn't* call 911, not yet.

Calling 911 would create quite the scene. Despite having starred on a television reality show, Maddy hated being the center of attention. Calling for emergency help—particularly during filming of a live broadcast—would bring unwanted attention. It would disrupt the competition and quite possibly stir a panic. Worse, it might reflect badly on the hotel. And it would most definitely ruin Genny's fun and her return among her peers.

Calling 911 would be her last resort, she firmly determined.

So now what?

She looked around, trying to find somewhere to hide. Rumor had it that the suite featured hidden spaces and a secret staircase or two. If this was spy headquarters in the original safe house, Maddy had no doubt there were built-in escape routes, but she hardly had time to search for them. By the time she found them, the men would have already found her. She had to think of something else, and she had to think fast.

She looked up, seeing the overhead cupola. Even if she could get up to the top, what then? Okay, so she saw a ladder there in the corner, and the windows appeared to open, but they opened onto the roof, at least five floors above the ground. She had done some crazy things in the past, including getting stuck on the flat roof of a building back home, but not even *she* was crazy enough to brave the many gables of the hotel!

Madison glanced back out the plate-glass window, to the great room four stories below. Maury, the rotten scoundrel, still sat with her grandmother. *He'd better not touch a hair on her head, or he'll have me to deal with ME.*

"These aren't plate-glass windows," Madison murmured in surprise. They were sliding doors. "I guess that's the reason for the half wall on the other side. What did they do?" she speculated aloud. "Dangle spies over the edge until they spilled their secrets?"

She thought she heard a clatter downstairs in the main suite. It could have just been the clatter of her heart, but Madison wasn't taking any chances. Making a hasty decision, she slid the window open just wide enough to squeeze through and hoped the narrow bit of floor beneath her feet was sturdy enough to hold her weight. She closed the window behind her, prayed the drapes fell back in place, and crouched low behind the half wall, the only thing that separated her from a deadly fall. The windows were the only thing that separated her from anyone inside the loft.

There were only a few inches of space between the two, but Maddy managed to turn around and lie on the cold strip of floor. Even if someone came into the upper room and gazed out the window to the great room below, they would have to peer down at their feet to notice her there. She prayed it didn't come to that.

Perched precariously on the narrow ledge— protected, yet still in grave danger—she could hear the competition as it unfolded below her. The sounds of life stirring below worked to calm her nerves. In time, she even thought to use the cell phone in her pocket. She didn't dare talk, lest she give away her position, but she could text. She found Sophie's phone number and sent a message to the innkeeper, saying that she had a delicate situation and needed Security in her suite, ASAP. She trusted the innkeeper would treat the situation with discretion, saving them all from an embarrassing ordeal.

# 17

It seemed to take forever, but she finally heard the security guard down below, calling her name. Still afraid someone might be in the loft, she kept still and sent another text, directing the guard to the loft.

Another several minutes, and she heard him come into the sitting area, cautiously calling her name. Only then did she struggle to her feet and work the window open.

"Ma'am, guests are forbidden on the ledges," the man began, his face set in a scowl.

"I certainly didn't do it for fun!" Madison cried, only halfway through the portal. "Could you give me a hand?"

Back on solid ground, she swiped the dust and grime from her clothes. So much for her pretty new blouse.

"Why were you out on the ledge, ma'am? This is highly irregular. I'm afraid I'll have to report this to management."

"Fine, you do that. I want to report someone breaking into my room."

The security guard went on full alert. "Someone broke into your room?"

Only then did Madison hesitate. Had they? Or had they given up after a few useless tries?

"Ah, could we go back down to discuss this?" Madison hedged.

"I suppose," he agreed, but with clear reluctance. "By the way, miss, why was your room barricaded? I had trouble getting in. That, you know, is a violation of fire safety code."

The back door leading to the deck was still barricaded, a fact that did not escape the man's attention. Maddy knew she was steadily racking up the violations. She wouldn't be surprised if Sophie didn't ask them to leave.

If neither of the doors had been tampered with, then obviously no one had broken in.

"I—I must have been mistaken," she said, turning to the guard with her apology. "Someone *was* trying to get in. He rattled the door several times and tried to break it down. I put the sideboard there to deter him and—" She realized how crazy she must sound, even before she saw the look upon his face.

To her surprise, he offered her a gentle smile. "Don't worry, ma'am. This isn't the first time this has happened."

"It isn't?"

"No, ma'am," he said, shaking his head. "People come here, read stories about the spies and secret spaces, hear some of the history behind the house, and they let their imaginations get the better of them. This is the first time someone has ever crawled out on the ledge, mind you, but it's not the first time someone thought they were being followed. I suspect it won't be the last, either."

"But you don't understand. There really was a man trying to get into our room."

"That happens, too, I'm afraid. Guests don't mean

any harm; they just want to see what the other rooms look like, especially this room. Some are searching for the hidden staircases or hoping to find a secret panel." He shook his head in wonder, apparently recalling some of the crazier stunts he had witnessed.

Madison decided not to press the issue. She knew there was more to it than her overactive imagination, but she had no proof. The men hadn't managed to get inside the room, so technically, no harm—and certainly no crime—had been committed. She thought it best to let the situation go.

"I'm sorry to have disturbed you," she said with a contrite expression.

"No problem, miss. I'll let Sophie know it was a false alarm. And if you'll promise to stay off the ledges, and to keep your exits clear, I won't mention the violations."

"I promise. Thank you."

"No problem, ma'am." He stopped to push the sideboard back into its proper place. "Let's leave this here, shall we? I hope the rest of your stay is less stressful. Enjoy your day." The guard tipped his hat and was gone.

After making certain the door clicked shut behind him, Madison sank onto the couch. She took a few moments to gather her wits, knowing Maury was still with her grandmother. She went to the bathroom and splashed cool water on her face. On a whim, she checked the closet to make certain the suitcase was still there and secure.

Her efforts were useless.

The suitcase was gone.


By the time she reached the great room, filming was over and Granny Bert once again chatted with the celebrity chef. Her poker friend was nowhere in sight.

Her grandmother took one look at her and propped her hands onto her hips. "What happened to you? You look like something the cat dragged up."

Madison glanced down at her dirty shirt, realizing she had forgotten to change. "Minor mishap. Granny, can I talk to you for a second?"

"We were just about to exchange recipes," the older woman huffed, clearly displeased with the interruption.

"I understand, Bertha, dear," the chef said, patting her hand tucked into the crook of his arm. "I have matters I must attend to myself, but I have your number. I'll call you later this evening. If you're free, perhaps we could have a nightcap."

"You call me," she agreed, without committing. She accepted the kiss he dropped onto her cheek, a giggle escaping her lips.

"Why, Granny," Madison teased, gently tugging on her grandmother's arm and pulling her away. "I do believe you're blushing."

"I've long been a fan of that man," she said, her gaze following him. "He's even more charismatic in person." Irritation moved into her face. "What was so all-fired important that you had to drag me away like that, anyway?"

"I saw Maury down here with you earlier. Do you know where he went?"

"How should I know? He got a phone call and said he had to go. He apologized and said he couldn't make our poker game, either. They were filming, so we weren't able to talk."

"He wasn't supposed to have his phone on him," Madison murmured, her tone somewhat reprimanding.

Her grandmother held up her own cell. "Well,

neither was I, but here it is. You're probably the only person in the room who followed the rules."

Judging from all the selfies and pictures being snapped around the room, her grandmother was probably right. "Never mind. It's just as well that he canceled the game. I don't want you around that man again."

"I was going to question him about the luggage."

"It doesn't matter anymore. It's gone."

"Gone?"

"Your friend Barton broke into our room and took it."

Her grandmother looked at her in alarm. "Did you tell the hotel?"

"Yes. Well, no, not that it was taken." She pushed out a weary sigh. "Long story. Let's find Genny, and I'll tell you both at one time."

"Can we do it over lunch? All those desserts were mighty tasty, but I'm coming down from a sugar rush and need something solid in my stomach."

"Don't worry. I can't wait to get out of here for a while."


They stayed out most of the afternoon. After a leisurely lunch, they did some sightseeing and visited a couple of local attractions. With the suitcase now out of their possession, they unanimously voted to forget the whole sordid incident. They would enjoy what was left of their trip and head home to Texas on Saturday morning.

"It's been fun, but I miss Brash and the twins," Madison admitted as they climbed the stairs back to their room. "And Megan."

"Cutter sounded so lonely when I talked to him this afternoon. He's been working some sort of new arson investigation, and I think it's really getting to him."

"Brash didn't go into details, but he mentioned something about it. Sounds like it's a bad situation."

"What about you, Granny Bert? Have you talked to Sticker since we've been gone?"

"Who?" Her manner was deliberately obtuse.

"Sticker. You know, the man who calls you his Belle. The man who took you to Vegas as his special guest when he won that lifetime achievement honor at the National Finals Rodeo. The one that follows you around like a lovesick hound dog. That man."

"Would that be the same man who was seen over at Wanda Shanks' house yesterday afternoon?" she asked coolly.

Genny laughed. "Cutter told me about that. Apparently, she left the door open when she was cleaning its cage, and Derron's parrot got loose. She couldn't get it back in and Derron was too busy to come home, so she called the fire department."

"First of all, why was *she* cleaning the cage? And second, how does that involve Sticker? He's too old to be on the fire department. A place would burn down by the time his creaking old joints got to moving. Too many years and too many falls off the back of bulls."

"Evidently, Derron pays her a little extra in with his rent if she'll clean his room. I guess that includes the bird's cage."

"No wonder he's in no hurry to move out," Madison said. "She even cooks for him."

"She enjoys having someone to fuss over," Granny Bert said. "Still doesn't explain what Sticker was doing over there."

"He went with Cutter to catch the bird. He even brought his lasso, but thank goodness, it didn't come to that. They put a bit of cheese in the cage, and the parrot went right in."

"Cheese? I never heard of such!" Madison laughed, topping the final flight of stairs. "Oh, my word! Is that my suitcase? It is! They returned my suitcase!" She rushed toward it, clapping her hands together in delight.

"I guess there's such a thing as honor among thieves, after all," Genny surmised.

Maddy happily pulled her suitcase into the suite. She unzipped it immediately, making certain everything was there. She hugged her favorite pair of boots to her. "I love these boots."

"Only because Gray hated them," Granny Bert reminded her. "Made you as tall as him."

"Brash doesn't mind them at all."

"I always said he was the bigger man."

"I don't think I'll wear this gown, though. I know for a fact they touched it." She wrinkled her nose at the thought of foreign hands on her lingerie. "Come to think of it, I may not wear any of this until I've washed it all."

"Well, you can't wear that blouse again. It's still filthy from your roll on the ledge this morning," Genny said, lifting the curtain to examine the small space. "Good thing it was you, and not me. My hips would have never fit." She peered down to the great room below. "They've already put out the wine and nibbles. I don't know about y'all, but I could go for a quiet dinner. Everyone suggests the *Iron Bridge Wine Company* just down the road. We could eat and come back for a nightcap by the fire."

"After the day I've had, a quiet night sounds nice."

"You two sound like a couple of old ladies," Granny Bert groused. "I've had livelier times at a quilting bee."

"You don't quilt," Madison reminded her.

"And that's why. Too boring for my tastes."

Genny watched the few people milling down below. "Mmm, I love that woman's pant suit. I wish my clothes fit me that well."

"Which one?" Madison nudged up to the window beside her friend.

"The tall blond. It's those killer long legs she has."

Maddy nodded in agreement. "She's the one I saw that first night, the one I mistook for the innkeeper. She waltzed into the room, looked around for like ten seconds, and breezed out again. See how she holds herself with an air of confidence? Like she owns the room. She must be an athlete of some kind. She's so poised and graceful."

"Maybe she's an actress. She looks like she could be in an action movie or something."

"Maybe she's working on a spy thriller and she's soaking in the ambiance of the house." She warmed to the idea as she spoke. "Maybe Beady Eyes Black Jacket is playing the part of the bad guy, and they're both here rehearsing."

"You and your code names," her friend snickered.

"Hey, it works, okay? Remember Trench Coat?" It was a name she had used for Caress Ellingsworth's killer, before she knew the person's real identity.

"How could I forget? You were nearly killed."

"I have had more than my fair share of brushes with death," Maddy agreed. "Who would think running a temporary agency could be so dangerous?"

"Not me. Ooh, and I see what you mean about seeing so well from up here. I can see someone outside on the deck, and another person coming down off the stairs."

Madison followed her line of sight. "That's odd," she said in surprise. "That's Barton down there on the deck. I thought he'd have checked out by now, after getting the suitcase he wanted so badly."

"*That's* Barton?"

"Yes. Why?"

"Because that's the man from the airport. He was the one with the little girl who gave you the note. I just assumed he was her father."

"No kids, or so he said," Granny Bert chimed in.

"This just keeps getting stranger and stranger," Madison said. She stepped back from the window, clearly upset.

"Want to know something even stranger? That blond woman just got a look at Barton and took off after him," Genny reported. "She'd better hurry, though. He just ran off."

# 18

Filming wrapped up the next day.

By that evening, a storm blew in. Temperatures dropped and snow flurries danced in the air, mingling with sleet. Wanting no part of the icy roads, the trio of Texans called for takeout and spent their last evening at *Peralynna* snuggled by the fire.

Madison and Genny ended up on the cuddle room sofa, curled up with glasses of wine and a shared plate of crackers, cheese, and fruit.

"I wish Granny Bert hadn't gone up so early. I feel guilty hanging out down here without her," Genny said.

"She'll never admit it, but I think she's a bit tired. And she'll deny this, too, but I bet she's talking to Sticker right this minute. Now that she knows he wasn't two-timing her with Miss Wanda, they're probably on speaking terms again."

"Do you think she'll ever marry him?"

"No. But I don't think she'll share him with anyone else, either," Maddy admitted.

Genny swirled the wine in her glass, mesmerized by its golden glow. "I can't believe I'm actually marrying Cutter. Just a few more days, and I'll be a married woman," she said softly.

Madison watched the warm light illuminating her friend's face. It appeared each time she spoke her fiancé's name. "Happy, much?"

"Delirious. Why didn't you tell me love could be like this?"

Madison studied her own wine, wrestling with the truth. "Because I didn't know," she admitted lowly. "Not until Brash."

"Why do you sound troubled by that?"

"Because I loved Gray, once upon a time. I truly did. I wouldn't have married him if I hadn't. We had some wonderful years together, and he gave me the twins. They're my world. But..."

Her friend finished the thought for her. "But you never loved him the way you love Brash."

"No. I had no idea love could even be like this, so heart and soul."

Genny nodded in agreement. "So complete." Her soft voice trembled with emotion. "And so absolutely terrifying."

"Terrifying?"

Again, she nodded. "That something could happen," she explained. "That I'll wake up and find this has all been some wonderful, glorious dream. That he'll come to his senses and wonder what it was he thought he saw in me. That—"

Maddy stopped her before she could go any further. "That you'll finally get your happily ever after. That, my friend, is nothing to be afraid of. Embrace it. Enjoy it. This is happening."

Genny's dimples reappeared. "It is, isn't it?" she said with a giggle. She even managed a little happy dance, without spilling a single drop of wine.

"It certainly is. And that man is crazy about you. We all knew it, long before either of you ever did."

Maddy's voice was smug.

"Just like everyone knew you and Brash would eventually get together. It took you long enough, but you finally managed it."

"You know what they say. Good things come to those who wait."

"Hear, hear."

The friends tipped their glasses together, happy smiles upon both their faces.

"Well, hello, you two." The innkeeper Sophie stopped for a visit. "Your grandmother isn't joining you this evening?"

"Not this evening," Maddy confirmed.

"It's a messy night out. Perfect for staying in by the fire." Sophie turned a pointed look toward Madison. "I trust today has been smoother than yesterday?"

Maddy's answer was slow in coming, as she debated how best to answer. She still hadn't told the innkeeper the whole truth, that someone had been in their suite and taken the suitcase. In the end, she simply smiled and said, "Yes. I'm sorry for any trouble I may have caused."

"Not to worry. I'm just glad it was a false alarm. All the same, I think perhaps we should lay off the spy stories tonight, don't you?"

They made the appropriate sounds of laughter. "By the way," Madison said, before Sophie moved along to greet new guests coming into the room, "I was wondering about one of your guests. A tall, blond woman, quite commanding with her presence. Do you know who I'm talking about?"

Sophie looked around. "Is she in here now?"

"No, I haven't seen her since last night. She wore a lovely dark-gray pantsuit. The first night we were here, she had on a navy blazer and a blue sweater."

"That would be Logan McKee. She's not a guest.

She works for one of the intel agencies."

Though spoken casually, the words slammed into Madison, catching her by surprise. She sucked in a tiny gasp as goose bumps scattered up and down her spine. She cut her eyes at Genny, who managed to squeak out, "Intel?"

It was more of a gulp, than a question. Obviously, Genny shared her unease.

"Yes," Sophie continued, waving her hand in a breezy manner. "She pops in and out quite often. With the NSA and so many other government agencies practically in our backyard, you never know who might be here at any given moment. We don't advertise the fact, but they often use the inn as a secure meeting location. It's even served as a safe house a time or two."

Madison's brow puckered in thought. "So, is this Logan McKee an agent?"

Sophie's laughter twinkled in the air. "I can hardly keep up with all the agencies, much less people's titles!" She waved to the couple approaching the pastry tray. "If you'll excuse me, I need to speak to Mr. and Mrs. Asano."

"Certainly," Madison murmured, her mind already miles ahead. She turned toward her friend, reluctant to voice her thoughts. "Genny, you don't suppose..."

Genny's blond head was already bobbing. "...that we somehow intercepted a piece of sensitive information?"

"Yes! It would make sense, you know. The note from the little girl, all those crazy letters and numbers, the case." She gasped and clutched her friend's arm. "The shadow from the chandelier! What if Logan McKee is a CIA agent, and that's some sort of coded message for her?"

"I don't know whether to be excited, or to be

frightened," Genny admitted.

"Why? They have the case back."

"But you still have the note."

Madison sucked in a sharp breath. Her voice was little more than a whisper. "That's right. I do." She felt around in her pocket and pulled out the crumpled piece of paper. "Do we really think this could be some sort of secret message? Some code?"

"I don't know. Hold it up to the light. Can you see anything?"

"I'm not sure. The paper is textured."

"No, look! Right along the edges of the petals! Aren't those letters?"

Madison brought the paper closer in for inspection, keeping it back-lit by the glow from the chandeliers. "I can't tell, but... yes. Yes, I think that's a 'k.' And an 'm, p, r.'" She frowned. "That doesn't make any more sense than those papers in the folders."

"Maybe they were the key, and this is the code," Genny suggested. "What are those letters written at the bottom, the ones that look like child's scribble?"

"Child's scribble," Maddy said wryly. "A backwards capital G, a capital L, capital J, and a lower-case p." She frowned as she studied the crude writing. "Or maybe just a circle with a stick behind it."

"Hmm. Wonder what it all means?"

"No idea. It doesn't even sound like something." She attempted to form a word from the general sounds of g, l, j, and p. It made no sense.

"Egypt?" Genny suggested.

"But what's the 'gl' sound?"

They tried several variations, none of them successful. Madison kept repeating the letters under her breath, hoping something would pop.

"Wait a minute!" A light bulb went off in her head. "GLJP."

"That's what we've been saying for thirty minutes."

"No, GLJP. That's it! Give me a pen and paper, and I'll show you."

Genny rooted around in her purse, finally coming out with a sales receipt and a pen. Madison drew the flower pattern she had doodled the day before, created from loopty-doops of the letters GLJP. It was, more or less, a match to the drawing on the paper.

"But if this is a code, why write the letters in plain view, right below it?" Genny wondered.

"Maybe it's a different sort of key. Maybe it tells you the order, and the direction, the code should be read. Read the G petals backwards, maybe starting at the bottom loop." She redrew them as she spoke. "The L and J the way you think, the P..." That one gave her pause, until she decided, "The P is lower case, so two loops, like this. It reads last, even though one of its loops comes before the G."

Genny slapped her friend on the arm. "You're brilliant! I think you're right. Hey, you should apply for a job with the CIA. You're good at this code thing, girlfriend."

"You forget, I raised twins. They spoke in their own code for the first few years of their lives."

"This all sounds quite logical, but we still have no idea what the message says."

"And I don't think I want to know," Madison was quick to say. "We should turn this over to the authorities."

Her phone buzzed with a text message.

"Probably Granny Bert," she said, digging her phone from her pocket.

Instead, she saw it came from the same number as before.

***You have something of ours.***

"Uh-oh." She turned the screen so Genny could

read the message.

"Act like you have no idea what they're talking about."

Her hands trembled as she typed her reply. **You have the case back. Now leave me alone.**

"I bet the black light is to read this note," Genny realized. Irrational as it was, they spoke in hissed whispers.

"You're probably right. Let's go back up. I don't like the idea of leaving Granny alone."

As their feet hit the first step, Madison's phone buzzed again.

**We want the note.**

They reached the second staircase.

**Clock is ticking.**

Fear seized Madison's heart. "That sounds like a threat."

Genny opened the door while Madison prepared a reply. Before she could finish typing, she received another message.

**No games. No cops.**

"Granny Bert? It's us," Genny called. "Granny Bert, where are you?" She walked through the suite as Madison's phone binged once again. "She must be in the bathroom."

"I don't think so," Madison said, her voice coming out strangled. She turned her phone toward her friend.

**We propose another trade.**

Below the message was a picture, this one of Granny Bert. Her hands, feet, and mouth were bound, and she lay in a deep pit.

# 19

"They have Granny Bert!"

Horrified, they gasped the words as one voice.

"Those dirty, rotten... who do they think they are, taking our grandmother?" Genny cried in outrage.

"I swear, if they hurt her..."

Hands trembling, as much with anger as with fear, Madison typed her message.

*What do you want?*

She didn't have long to wait. Her phone binged with the reply.

*We get note, you get location of your spitfire.*

Despite the dire circumstances, Madison couldn't help but smile. "I'm sure she's more than they bargained for."

*Where and when?* She typed.

*Hotel in 30. NO COPS.*

Genny paced the floor. "What are we going to do?"

Madison enlarged the image on her phone. Something about the surroundings seemed so familiar...

"I know where this is!" she said excitedly. "This is the old cotton mill. I remember seeing this pit." She grabbed her coat and stuffed her arms inside. "Come on, we're going to get her!"

"But what if they're watching us?"

BECKI WILLIS

"They're obviously not at the hotel, if they want to meet us in thirty minutes." Madison slung her purse onto her shoulder and was already halfway to the door.

"What if we pass them on the road?"

"Good point. Let's find Sophie."

They raced down the stairs, heedless to the stares that followed them into the great room. Sophie was still there, visiting with guests.

Madison ran up to her and tugged on her arm, even as she apologized. She pulled the sputtering woman aside, unconcerned now about making a scene. Her voice was breathless and her sentences ran together as she spoke quickly.

"I'm sorry! I'm sorry, truly I am, but I don't have time to explain. I lied to you earlier. It wasn't my overactive imagination. Someone broke into my room and stole something, and now they've taken my grandmother. I can't call the police or they'll hurt her. I need to borrow your car or the hotel's van or something they won't recognize, and I need you to call your friend Logan McKee and tell her I'm headed to the old cotton mill that's now an antique mall. Tell her it's a matter of life and death and please stop staring at me like I'm crazy and just DO IT! Give me the keys to your car!"

"I—I can't," the innkeeper stammered. "It's in the shop, and it's against company policy to allow you to drive the van." She saw the thunderous light that came to both women's eyes and quickly added, "But I can have Percy drive you wherever you need to go. Just give me a minute."

"We don't have a minute! We have to go NOW!" Madison took off running, pulling the innkeeper along with her.

Genny did damage control, apologizing to the

152

stunned onlookers. "Sorry! Family emergency!" She was right on their heels.

"Percy, there's no time for explanations, just take these ladies where they want to go."

His eyes fell upon Genny and he broke out in a smile. "Why, certainly. What—"

"Not now, Romeo," Genny said, grabbing his arm. "Come on!"

"Call your friend," Madison said over her shoulder, "but do *not* call the police. Promise me." Her eyes bore into the innkeeper's.

"I—I promise."

"The old cotton mill. Call her!" she barked as she backed out the door.

"The antique mall complex?" Percy asked, more than a little confused, but happy to have Genny still tugging on his arm. He'd go anywhere she led.

"Yes. Get us there as fast as you can."

"I know a short cut."


Percy claimed it was a shortcut, but to Madison, it seemed to take forever.

The businesses were closed for the evening. Even though the buildings glowed from within, the complex was dark when they arrived, bathed more in shadow than in light. Security lamps offered random pools of light, the only thing pushing back against the black cover of night. Only the wind stirred. The light mist from earlier had given way to tiny shards of ice falling from the sky.

The ice bit into Madison's skin as she jumped from the van. Seeing the property lit at night, she realized how massive the complex was. A pit formed in her belly. Finding her grandmother wouldn't be as simple as she thought.

She turned back only long enough to address their driver. "Percy, you know what to do."

Eyes large with fright, the man nodded his head. "I have both your numbers. I'll text if I see anyone." His eyes darted into the night and skittered away without meeting Genny's gaze. With clear reluctance, he gulped and made a half-hearted attempt at gallantry. "I—I could go with you."

"No. Stick to the plan. You're our lookout."

Obviously relieved, Percy reached into the floor behind him. "Don't forget the rope."

Percy carried a length of rope and chains in the back of the van, necessities for ice-slick roads and snowy terrain. The chain was too heavy for the women to carry, but Genny hoisted the rope coil onto her shoulder and quietly shut the door behind them. While Percy found a darkened parking space with optimum line of sight, Madison and Genny slipped into the shadows that edged the old structure.

"What did you say this place was?" Genny whispered, eying the massive building on their right. Made partially of stone, partially of brick, she imagined it would be intriguing in the daylight. At night, under these circumstances, it was overwhelmingly large and oppressive.

"An old textile mill, turned into a neat assortment of shops and restaurants," Madison answered, keeping her voice low. While en route, she studied a map of the complex and committed it to memory. It took a moment now to get her bearings, but after a moment of contemplation, Madison pointed to the huge stone and brick building. "This is the Carding Building. We need the backside of Old Weave, the next building over."

Percy had deposited them at the side of the complex, rather than front and center where they would be more easily seen. The drive narrowed into little more than a paved alley. Madison started down it, staying closer to the tree line than to the grassy knoll sloping down from Carding. "I think I can make out the old smoke stack ahead, so we're headed in the right direction. I recognized the pit where Granny is. We saw it when we were on the decking near the zip line place, around back."

Few lights illuminated their path. The women moved stealthily through the darkness, not knowing what—or who—awaited them. As they passed beneath a dimly lit portico, cluttered with the overflow from its attached business, Genny dared another comment. "This place may be neat during the day, but it's spooky as heck at night. What is that noise? Is that the wind?"

"I think it's the river. It's just down there." Madison flung her hand to her right.

They cleared the portico and Genny glanced through the barren trees. A weak hint of moonlight filtered through the clouds and naked limbs, offering a ghostly glow to the thin ribbon of water. "Is that another building down there?"

"The ruins, I think, of the old power house." Madison felt her phone vibrate and pulled it from her pocket, slowing just long enough to read the text. "Sophie says her friend is on the way. Still no sign of the men."

"Uh, Maddy." The worry in Genny's voice pulled Madison's eyes to her friend. Genny motioned ahead. "Our road just ran out. Now what?"

Stuffing her phone back into her pocket, Maddy puffed out a resigned sigh. "We hit the dirt. But be careful. The ground looks pretty rough."

Advancement was slow. Without pavement, the uneven ground was littered with sticks, briers, stones, and more. A steep embankment fell sharply to their left and tumbled its way down to the water.

It required careful footing and great concentration not to fall with the slope. Icy needles rode on the wind, further impeding their progress. The wind tossed hair into their eyes and made their toes and unprotected fingers go numb. Neither were dressed for an excursion in the elements.

Nor was Granny Bert. The knowledge drove the women deeper along the dark path.

"Maddy," Genny whispered again. "We're going down, not up. The building is up there."

"I can see that," Madison hissed. Nerves made her snap at her friend. "If you can't say something positive, just don't say anything."

The Old Weave building was in front of them, perched high above where they currently stood. A maze of pilings served up the deck towering three stories above their heads, but even in the darkness, they could see getting closer would be difficult.

"While I was on that deck, I could see the pit down below," Madison recalled. "Part of the deck is cut out to overlook the old brickwork and the drainage pipes. I think that's where they're holding Granny Bert."

"This is where I don't mention the high rail fence with spiky tops and the thick hedges surrounding it," Genny pointed out. Lighting from the deck made it easier to see the obstacles that lay before them. "But I will mention I see another option. I think that's an old stone fence up there. Or maybe it's a retainer wall. Either way, no spiky tops."

"Let's go."

The ground rose on an incline. Soggy piles of leaves and fallen limbs, slick with ice pellets, made the path treacherous. The women crawled over the ancient barrier, pushing and tugging one another until they both scaled the crumbling stones. The ground on the other side was slightly more stable.

"What is that?" Genny asked. In the darkness, an odd silhouette rose before them and looked strangely out of place.

"Part of the zip line."

"So, here's something positive. There's enough light back here that I can see sidewalks and another parking lot. Looks like we could have driven right up to the back."

Madison shot her friend a dark frown. "The negative is, we didn't know that until now. We took that obstacle course for nothing."

"Maybe not. Look, this way goes up under the deck. This may lead us right to Granny Bert!" Though still a whisper, her voice rose with excitement.

Considered part of the complex grounds, no trees or fallen limbs littered the path on this side of the fence, but the earth was still uneven. It swelled and fell in a gentle slope. Even with the dim spill of light from nearby lamps, they could see the shallow draining ditch leading under the deck.

Madison ran the last few yards, trying not to stumble in her haste. But as she neared the sunken area beneath the deck, disappointment stung sharp and deep.

"This isn't a pit at all!" she wailed, realizing her error. "It's completely open on one side!" She dropped her face into her hands and fought back a sob. "I thought I knew exactly where she was. Now we have to start all over!"

"Let me see that picture again."

While Genny studied the photo in the message, Madison paced the small area she had mistaken as a pit. From above, she had seen only three walls, all made of stone or brick, and one of them draped with pipes and valves. She incorrectly assumed that the fourth wall was directly beneath her and out of her line of vision. She never dreamed that it didn't exist at all.

"I think this could still be nearby," Genny said. "Look at the brickwork. It looks like this. And those pipes and gages are a lot like these. Sure, some of them are much bigger, but some look just like this."

"And like old pipe everywhere. I can't believe I led us on a wild goose chase! Think of all the valuable time I cost us! What if—"

"You're getting a message," Genny broke in, turning the phone toward her. Her eyes were large. "It's them."

As much from cold as from nerves, Madison's hands trembled as she clumsily reclaimed her phone and read the simple text.

*At hotel.*

"They're there," she breathed. "What do I say?"

"Stall. I'll text Sophie."

Blowing on her fingers to coax them into working, Madison typed out her message. *Be right down.*

Looking up from her own phone, Genny said, "I told Sophie to create a diversion. Maybe it will buy us some time."

Madison went back to pacing, even though the area was small and uneven. Her hands worried her hair. "I don't know, Gen," she fretted. "Now what? Where else could she be? I was so sure she was here at the mill."

"What about the old ruins? It's the perfect place to hide someone. I'm sure no one goes down there much, especially not in the dead of winter."

"That's it! That's perfect!" Hope glittered in Maddy's hazel eyes. "It looks like this building, because it's part of the same complex! Come on, we need to hurry."

"Hold on. Let me text Sophie and ask her if all three men are there. With any luck, they left Granny Bert alone and we can use our flashlights. I don't relish the idea of rolling head-first into the river."

"I'm not waiting for the answer," Madison warned. She tucked her hands beneath her armpits to warm them and stepped back into the elements. Without the protection of the overhead decking, sharp bits of ice mixed with snow slapped her in the face. "Here, let me carry the rope. We still might need it."

They retraced their path, scampering over the old stone fence and down the slippery slope that led to the river. From there, they trekked to their right, hoping it was more direct. Being further from the sparse security lights around the building, it was a darker path, and therefore more treacherous. Every so often, Maddy used the flashlight app on her phone to guide the way.

"Watch your step," she warned. "There's some sort of low wall up ahead, with tin on top of it. Must be a well or pit of some kind."

After pausing to read a text, Genny hurried to keep up. The terrain was too risky to read and walk at the same time. "Sophie says Barton is the only one asking for you, but she sees a black jacket through the window, so she assumes someone is guarding the back. No word on Maury, so he could be here."

"We'll have to assume he's guarding Granny Bert and be as quiet as possible. Here, let's go this way."

Maddy took a step forward and fell off the face of the earth.

# 20

"Tell me again," Megan said. "Why am I wearing this horrible shirt and this black eyeliner?"

"Hey, watch it. That's *my* shirt," Blake said in offense.

"I know. It's two sizes too big for me and it's some advertisement for a *race* track." The disdain was clear in her voice.

"It looks great on you," Bethani assured her best friend. "Now put this hoodie on."

"Are you kidding me? You already made me change into my old black framed glasses and wear this black junk on my eyes. Now you want me to cover my hair? It took me a half hour to get this look. It was going to look great with my new shirt and my red boots, but you made me change those, too. What is wrong with you tonight?" Megan demanded.

"We're going to hang out with some new friends."

"Dressed like thugs?"

"We want to fit in," Blake muttered.

Tonight, he was driving. Mr. de even loaned them his new pickup. The twins talked to their mother this afternoon, finally convincing her to allow them to drive to Riverton. They wisely omitted mention of the bonfire, mentioning only dinner at *Dairy Queen*.

Madison knew how fond her son was of the food there, or anywhere, when it came down to it.

"Wait a minute. Where is my friend and what have you done with her?" Megan demanded, looking suspiciously at the other girl. "I love you to death, sista, but you're a bit of a snob. You're just now getting used to cowboys. No way you've suddenly become friends with thugs."

"Okay, okay. You got me. We're doing a favor for Derron. It's a job, actually. He's paying me by finding me a dress for prom."

"Which he was probably going to do anyway," Megan pointed out. "You do realize the man has played you."

Bethani frowned, just now considering that possibility. "Maybe, but it's for a good cause. We're trying to help a new friend of ours."

"You've got two minutes to explain, or I'm getting out of this truck at the next stop sign."

"Her name is Tasha, and she's really cool. She and Blake have something going. She—"

"We do not!" her brother broke in with a protest.

"You've been texting each other for two days and you have that goofy smile on your face. Look on the bright side. If she likes *you* now, that means she doesn't like thimble-brain Frankie." She whipped back toward her friend, her hair slapping Blake in the face. Tonight, her hair was long and straight, and slightly stringy beneath her black hoodie. "Her mom died a couple of years ago and her dad is always working. Her home life has gone down the drain and she's started hanging out with some real losers, mostly because her best friend Angela moved to Austin and her other best friend Kaitlyn has a new boyfriend and doesn't have time for her. Promise me that will never happen to us."

"Promise."

"Even if that new guy at school asks you out?"

"Even then."

Satisfied, Bethani continued with her tale. "So, her dad is worried about her and hired *In a Pinch* to follow her around and report back to him. Only it would look weird for Derron to follow her around, even though we know he's not into young girls. Or girls of any age, but that's beside the point. He asked me to check into her, and I did, and I found out she's pretty cool, just lonesome and confused and about to make a really big mistake by falling in with this group." Bethani paused long enough to draw in a deep breath. "So basically, we're going to save her from herself."

The most pressing question Megan thought to ask was, "And *when* did all of this happen? I help my mom for *one* day and you go all Columbo on me!" her friend wailed.

"So, are you in?"

Like a true best friend and soon-to-be sister, Megan never hesitated. "Of course."

"Great. Here's your hoodie."


They pulled into the back of the *Dairy Queen* parking lot, nosing their way into a small cluster of other vehicles. Most of them were older, junkier models. Many had dents. Some had multi-colored panels. Blake was careful to keep Mr. de's shiny new pickup well away from the threat of opening doors and any contagious rust that might be floating through the air.

"Hey, my friend, you made it!" one of the guys said, bumping fists with Blake. "And you brought a new chick! Well played."

"Hey, girl." Freddy sidled up to Bethani, pushing his way between her and her friend. "Glad you made it." He fingered her long hair and offered what he probably thought was a charming smile. Bethani thought it looked more like a leer. "I didn't know you were a blond. I like."

She resisted jerking away from his touch. "This is my friend Megan."

"Hey, girl. What's up?"

"The moon," she replied dryly.

Another boy snickered and pushed forward from where he lounged against the front of an old Chevy truck, puffing on a cigarette. The crowd parted, clearly deferring to him as their leader. "I'm Julio," he said, stopping in front of Megan. "You can ride with me."

She gave him a scathing look. "I don't think so."

He merely grinned, taking it as a challenge. He winked and dropped his cigarette, grinding it out at her feet. "Somebody order grub." He barked the instructions over his shoulder. "Let's eat. Then we can get the real party started."

Two of the other boys disappeared to do his bidding. Julio kept his eyes on Megan as the rest of the group made small talk and laughed at each other's lame jokes. Megan inched her way between Bethani and the creep named Frankie, but she could never quite escape the leader's brooding gaze. By the time the food arrived, he cornered her and insisted she join him on the tailgate. Bethani came along, which meant Frankie squeezed in, as well.

Julio was the first one finished. Even though the girls and a couple of the guys had most of their burgers left, he wadded up his trash, jumped from the truck, and declared dinner was over. He turned on his heel and swung his arm in a wide arc. "Let's go," he said.

Blake tugged on Tasha's arm. "Why don't you ride with us, and show us the way?"

"Cool."

It was a four-door pickup, but they all piled into the front seat. Megan and Bethani shared a seatbelt, squeezing into a space meant for one.

"You two have enough room?" Tasha asked, pretending to move closer against Blake for the girls' sake.

"Plenty," Bethani assured her. "Where's this bonfire we're going to, and what are we going to do? Make s'mores?"

"I doubt it. Knowing Julio and Freddy, they're going to blow something up." She rolled her eyes and muttered something beneath her breath, something that sounded a lot like 'idiots.'

"How long have you known those guys?"

"Long enough," she said with a shrug. "But I just started hanging with them about a month ago."

"I just wondered," Bethani said, her voice hesitant. "Because... you don't seem to fit in with them, you know?"

Tasha stiffened, but Blake gave her a gentle nudge. "That's a good thing, not an insult."

"Oh."

"Is Julio always such a jerk?" Megan asked. "He was all like 'me cave man, you woman.' I thought he might club me over the head and drag me off by the hair."

"He was actually on his best behavior tonight. You should see him some nights, all moody and quiet. Goes off by himself and sulks."

"If he's such a jerk, why do you hang with him?" Blake asked.

Tasha shrugged, her eyes downcast. "It's not like I

have a bunch of other options. It's better than sitting at home alone." She glanced up and motioned with a black fingernail. "Turn up here."

They followed the small line of cars out of town and down a dirt road. As they crossed a long wooden bridge, the cars in front of them slowed so they could toss empty beer cans out their windows.

"Bookerman's Bridge?" Blake guessed.

"The one and only."

Feeling increasingly uncomfortable, the misfits, plus one, continued down the road until the vehicles ahead turned into a lane clearly marked 'Private.'

"Where are we?" Bethani asked.

"Some old warehouse," Tasha said. "It used to be an oil field service, but it's been empty for a while."

"Is this where the bonfire is? I don't see it."

"Just wait. You'll see it soon enough."

Tasha got out on Blake's side, as the other two girls slid from the passenger's side. "I don't have a good feeling about this," Bethani whispered to Megan. "Stay close."

Over Tasha's purple-streaked head, Blake sent his sister a loaded look. They could still communicate without saying a word.

"We don't have to stay long," Tasha offered.

"Sounds like a plan."

There were only two other girls at the bonfire, and a half-dozen boys. Bethani tried to keep their names straight but found it easiest to think of the boys as Jerk 1, Jerk 2, and Jerk 3. Even though they were the biggest jerks of all, she knew Freddy and Julio by name. Another boy was called Smokes.

One of the girls, a black girl named Nae Nae, came up to where the twins huddled with Megan and Tasha. The wind had picked up, making the night air feel even colder, particularly on the rise where they stood.

The warehouse sprawled below them in a lower field.

"This is going to be awesome," she said excitedly. "This is the last trial run. Julio thinks he has it down now."

Blake gave Tasha a quizzical look, but she avoided eye contact.

"Where's the bonfire?" Megan asked.

"Right there," Nae Nae said with a jerk of her head.

Her friends moved about in the dark, busy circling the old building and talking among themselves. The wind carried their voices in the other direction, making it hard to hear what they said.

"All I see is the building."

"Well, *duh*." Shaking her head, Nae Nae muttered something beneath her breath and stalked off to find the others.

A flame sparked in the distance, near the back of the massive structure. Another flared to life on the right side of the old warehouse, immediately followed by one on the left. High-pitched laughter caught and carried on the wind, their torches blazing as they ran through the darkness. The red-haired girl stumbled and let out a long string of curse words, demanding that Nae Nae help her. The pair staggered back to the hill with the others as Julio quietened the group and made his announcement.

"I figure we have no more than fourteen minutes between the first charge and when the first fire engine arrives. Django, you timing us?"

Jerk 2 held up a stopwatch and whooped.

"Sher, you and Bobby are lookouts. Nae Nae, you serve the beer. Moon Girl can help you." He winked at Megan. He turned back around, assuming she would jump to do his bidding. He cupped his hands over his mouth and called to the lone boy still down by the warehouse. "Ready, Smokes? Fire in the hole!"

The wind was against them, but a voice floated out from the darkness. "Fire in the hole!"

A loud boom rent the night air, throwing flames into the dark sky and shaking the very ground where they stood. Bethani lost her footing and almost tumbled off the hill, but Tasha and Blake helped her back up. While the other kids hollered and whooped with glee, the frightened twins and Megan turned on their new friend.

"What the hel—heck is going on?" Blake demanded.

"Their idea of fun," Tasha said sheepishly.

The echo of the boom died away, but the crackle and hiss of fire took its place. With the wind's help, the flames burned hot and high.

"Did you see that? Did you freaking see that?" Smokes screamed in excitement, running back to meet his friends. While he and the other guys exchanged chest bumps, Blake grabbed his sister and Megan's hands.

"We're getting out of here. Now." He shoved them toward the truck and turned back for Tasha. "You coming with us, or you staying with these losers?"

She looked over her shoulder, at the eight kids who had just set a warehouse on fire. It was the first time she had actually seen them in action. She thought their claims of arson were nothing but empty bravado and false posturing.

"I'm coming with you!" she said, joining them in a race for the truck.

"Hey, you get back here!" Julio cried, seeing the group defecting. He took it as a personal insult. He shook his fist and started up the hill, spittle flying from his mouth and disappearing into the wind. "Nobody leaves until I say so, you got that?" He stalked toward them, but Blake and the girls quickened their pace. They took off at a run, making it to the truck before the others could stagger up the hill and charge the truck.

# 21

She seemed to fall forever.

Despite her own warning just seconds earlier, Madison let out a loud scream and rolled head over heels down the side of the hill.

"Maddy! Maddy, are you okay?" Genny scrambled to the edge of the drop-off, trying to determine the best path down. She used her flashlight to search for her friend but saw nothing. Her voice, low but stern, took on a no-nonsense tone. "Talk to me, Madison Josephine Cessna Reynolds, so I know you're still alive!"

Upon further investigation, Genny realized it wasn't a low wall Maddy had seen, covered with tin. It was an entire building, backed up to the embankment with only its tin roof visible from above. It was built at river level and most likely used as a storage shed for machinery, meaning her friend had taken a long and nasty fall. Her voice turned frantic. "Maddy, talk to me!" she begged.

Madison's voice was strangled and weak, but it carried above the sound of the river. "Alive," she croaked from somewhere below.

"I'm coming down."

Bracing her hand on the rusted tin of the building's roof, and her foot against the crumbling brick exterior, Genny more or less climbed down the side of the old building. She clung to a nearby sapling for support when she could, and half-crawled, half-fell the rest of the way to the ground. Scrambling to her feet, she softly called for her friend again.

"Down here."

By the time Genny reached her friend, Madison had struggled into a sitting position, examining her arms and legs for open wounds and broken bones. Finding neither, she removed sticks and leaves from her hair.

"Are you okay?" Genny squealed, not bothering to censure her volume.

"Been better."

"Did you break anything?" When she attempted to rise, Genny shook her hands. "Don't get up just yet. Take a minute to gather yourself."

"This ground is cold and wet. Help me up."

It took two efforts, a mumbled curse or two, and quite a few grunts and groans, but Madison was finally on her feet. "I lost the rope," she realized. "We need to find it."

"I'll go back."

A few feet away, Genny stumbled across the coil of rope. Literally. She caught herself just before falling. "Found it."

"Shh," Madison said. "Listen."

They cocked their heads, straining to hear over the sounds of the river and the wind. It was faint, but the sound came again. A shrill whistle, somewhere nearby.

"Granny Bert!" Madison cried with relief.

"How do you know?"

"Don't you remember the signal? My grandparents

used that pattern—two long, five short—as a call for help. Grandpa Joe taught me that if I was ever lost in the woods, or needed help, to use that same code. Holler, whistle, honk the horn, whatever it took. Two longs, five short. Granny Bert used it when she called us in from riding our bikes. Don't you remember?"

"Oh, yeah, I do," Genny said, breaking into a grin. "She used to blow the car horn. If we didn't hear the horn, we heard all the dogs barking!"

"Thank the Lord, she's alive!" Until now, Madison hadn't allowed herself to think the alternative. Sheer relief made her legs weak, more so than any twenty-foot tumble. "That black glob in the shadows must be the old power house. I think the sound came from there."

"We should still be careful," Genny cautioned. "She may be able to whistle, but that doesn't mean that Maury guy isn't somewhere nearby. He may have heard you scream."

A sound made them both freeze. A stick snapped in the darkness, followed by the rustle of leaves. Someone, or something, was in the woods with them.

Madison put a cautioning hand on her friend's arm. The women barely dared to breathe as they shrank back against the slim trunk of a tree. The sound shuffled again in the leaves, and something white glowed in the night. Glancing down at their own attire, Madison breathed a sigh of relief that she and Genny both wore dark colors. Maury's white shirt peeked from his coat, making it easy to track his progress as he moved between them and the storage shed.

Feeling a stone beneath her feet, Genny carefully bent to retrieve it. She didn't need to tell Madison the thoughts running through her mind. As usual, they were on the same wavelength. Tossing it as hard as she could, Genny threw the rock well in front of the man who searched for them. When he hurried his pace, traveling away from the women, they moved stealthily through the darkness, inching closer to the abandoned power house.

Calling on long-forgotten softball skills, Madison launched another stone, hers sailing even further than Genny's.

"Show off." Genny barely breathed the word aloud, but it earned a crinkled nose from her friend.

Granny Bert whistled again, the coded rhythm confirming her presence in the old ruins.

As Maury moved closer to the storage shed, the women moved closer to the massive structure that once produced water-generated power for the old mill. Close enough now to make out details amid the thick night shadows, they soon discovered another problem. Built directly upon pilings planted deep in the river, the ground floor of the old structure was well above their heads. They needed to find an entry point, quickly and quietly.

"One more rock," Genny whispered, hoping to keep Maury occupied long enough for them to find a way in. She heaved another stone, but it hit an unseen tree and landed with a thud, much too close for comfort.

A brief flash of light, probably from his cell phone, shot across the woods as Maury turned toward the sound. Genny gulped, and Madison reached for another stone, this one heavier than the others. She pulled back her arm and threw it with all her might.

They never knew if it was the stone or a falling limb, but something clattered atop the tin roof of the dilapidated shed. It made a resounding racket in the night. Something else creaked and gave way. A loud crash echoed through the hollowed building.

While Maury undoubtedly turned and rushed to the shed, Madison and Genny rushed toward the power house, less concerned now with making a racket of their own. They found the opening they hoped for, helped each other over the trash and litter of fallen brick and crumbled iron, and stepped into the ruins.

# 22

"Get in! Get in!"

Blake yelled at the girls as they ran for the safety of the truck. Fire crackled in the night sky and the acrid scent of smoke burned their nostrils.

He didn't wait for seatbelts. The minute he heard Bethani's door click shut, Blake gunned the motor and the truck lurched forward. For one awful moment, he thought he was stuck in the sandy soil, but he slowly turned the wheels. Dirt flew in all directions. The tires spun as they found traction and the truck fishtailed out of the drive.

Behind them, an enraged Julio railed in anger and threw his blazing torch after them. It barely missed the truck, but from his rearview mirror, Blake saw it fall to the ground, bounce, and tumble. It rolled toward the other vehicles, leaving a trail of fire in its wake.

Blake threw on his brakes. Without the aid of seatbelts, everyone flew forward, himself included. While the girls grabbed for the dash and Megan complained of a jammed finger, Blake opened his door.

"Call 911," he told Tasha. When she hesitated, he prodded her into action with his elbow. "Do it!" he barked

"Where—Where are you going?" Bethani asked.

"I've gotta go help them. If that fire spreads beneath the cars, they'll all blow."

Bethani grabbed her brother's arm. "Wait! Don't go!"

His face was pale, but his jaw set with determination. "I have to, Beth. It's the right thing to do."

"Be careful!" All three girls chimed as one.

Blake took off at a run, calling for the other boy to help him. "Come on, Julio! We have to move these cars!"

The warehouse fire raged behind Julio as the fire from the torch smoldered before him. Neither was a match for the rage boiling inside the rebel teen. Blinded by anger, Julio did not understand.

"Get away from my ride, man! Smokes! Django! He's stealing our cars!"

Not wasting precious moments with explanations, Blake jerked open the door of the first vehicle, hoping the keys were in the ignition. As he started the motor, Julio ripped the door from his hand and pulled Blake out by the collar of his shirt. The angry teen punched Blake in the stomach.

"Nobody steals from me!" Julio yelled. "And nobody, I mean *nobody*, walks away from me!" His next punch landed in Blake's unprotected face.

Before the ragtag team's leader could hurl his third punch, one hundred and ten pounds of blond fury launched onto his back. Bethani flung herself upon the boy and hooked her legs around his waist, leaving her hands free to pound his head and pull on his hair.

"What the—you crazy girl! Get off me!" Julio straightened and spun, crushing the girl between him and the car, but Bethani refused to release her hold.

She dug her fingers into his neck and tugged, kneeing him like a horse until he staggered forward.

"Go, Blake! Move the car!" she called over her shoulder. She kneed Julio again for good measure.

A bit dazed from the attack, Blake slung the hair and the blood from his face and jumped back in the car, pulling it forward. Only then did he notice that Megan had already pulled one of trucks to safety and was running for another.

"Go back, Megan!" Blake yelled. He barely took time to put the car in park. He wasn't sure he killed the motor. He only knew that Megan was feet away from disaster.

The auburn-haired girl was already in the front seat. Blake ran toward her, frantically waving his arms. "Don't start it!" he yelled. "Don't start it! Put it is neutral and get out! Get out now!"

Megan couldn't see it, but the fire was almost beneath the truck she sat in, the flames licking at the back tires. If she started the motor, exhaust from the engine would combust and the truck would surely explode. Blake couldn't let that happen.

"Get out! Put it in neutral and get out!"

Confused, Megan slipped the gear into neutral but kept her foot on the brake. She opened the door to ask what he meant, her hand poised on the keys. As Blake raced by, he jerked her arm and flung her unceremoniously to the ground. She hit the grass hard but came up with fire in her eyes and spit on her tongue.

Her eyes widened when she saw the real fire, at eye level, moving toward her. Fast. Megan scrambled to her feet and ran, vaguely aware of Blake putting himself between the flame and the tailgate.

"Blake!" she screamed. "Come on!"

Using all his strength, Blake gave the truck a

mighty push. It rolled forward and down a slight incline. Blake didn't stand around to watch its slow descent across the pasture and into the nearby fence. He felt the scorch of fire against his jeans and turned to run, heading for the next vehicle.

Freddy stepped in front of him, sliding behind the wheel of a beat-up Camaro. "Thanks, man. You saved our asses."

Without another word, he turned the key, gunned the engine, and shot off into the night, barely giving his passenger time to close the door.

Finally free of the blond latched onto his back, Julio refused to be as gracious. He spat obscenities into the wind and stormed away without another word.

Tasha found a fire extinguisher in Brash's truck and ran to help her new friends. While Bethani and Megan kicked dirt onto the fire left by the torch, Blake ruined a pair of boots as he stomped out the flames. For the first time, he was thankful his sister insisted he wear his oldest pair tonight.

Between the four of them, they fought the secondary fire down to a smolder. There was no hope for the fire raging in the warehouse below. As the rebel teens responsible for the fiasco turned tail and ran, Blake and the girls made certain the danger was minimal until the fire department could arrive.

Just before the Riverton VFD arrived on scene from the north, Blake pulled onto the blacktop road, headed south.


It was a long drive back to The Sisters. The teens passed two firetrucks on the way. Blake recognized Cutter driving one of the engines.

"We have to tell."

"We are so dead."

"Grounded for life."

"Goodbye, freedom. Hello, misery."

"You could've been hurt."

"You, too."

"You, three."

"And what was that about, jumping on Julio's back like that?"

"I didn't even get in my own punch."

"Don't sulk, bro. You're still the hero of the night."

"You'll have a shiner by morning."

Still squashed between her new friends, Tasha's voice was small as she broke into the glum conversation. "Do we really have to tell?"

"Yes."

"We have to tell."

"We'll all do it together."

# 23

"Granny! Where are you?" Madison and Genny hissed the words as they entered the old ruins.

Hearing no reply, they moved further inside. The weak, watery light of the moon, echoed by the river beyond, gave the concrete beneath their feet a pale and ghostly glow. Wind howled through the glassless windows and rushed down the pipes and broken bricks, whirling about the gutted building with eerie moans. As their eyes adjusted to the deeper shadows inside, they made out a few scant details. Huge, circular pieces of equipment. Massive boilers and extensive pipes. A long piece of grated metal—perhaps once structural support, perhaps scaffolding—hung suspended in the air, a dark skeleton amid the shadows.

"Granny Bert! Where are you?" Madison called, daring to raise her voice above a whisper.

They heard a muffled voice, and the sound of movement. Staying close to one another, they hurried as best they could through the jumble of industrial, natural, and man-made waste. They entered another room of the ruins, heard Granny Bert's low whistle, and found still two more sectional spaces before spotting her.

Granny Bert lay on the floor of the old building, trussed up like a turkey on Thanksgiving Day. Her legs were bound at the ankles, her hands tied behind her back. The binding around her mouth glowed the brightest of all. She mumbled something unintelligible as the women dropped to their knees beside her.

As Genny knelt to untie her feet, Maddy made quick work of the gag around her mouth.

"Granny, are you okay? We were so worried! Are you hurt? Is anything broken? Your face is bleeding!" Madison spoke in a rush, not waiting for her grandmother's reply to any of her questions.

Despite the blood smeared across her cheek, the bindings still on all four limbs, and the bone-chilling cold surrounding them in the ruins, the old woman managed a smile. "Been better." They were Maddy's exact words from ten minutes earlier. Her voice was gruffer than usual but came out strong, considering her circumstances. "Cut my face on that wire, trying to loosen the gag enough to whistle."

"Thank goodness you did! I heard Grandpa Joe's emergency code and knew it was you." Madison gave her grandmother a jubilant hug.

Still working on the ropes at the older woman's feet, Genny looked up in frustration. She kept her voice low, but her annoyance was clear. "I can't get these loose! Find me something to use as a saw."

"I don't know if we have time. Maury could be back at any moment," Madison worried.

"Well, I can't hop out of here like a bunny," Granny Bert snorted. "Unless you plan on carrying me out, you've got to cut me free."

While Genny used a rusted piece of tin to saw through a few fibers, at best, Maddy worked on freeing her grandmother's hands. Granny Bert groaned as circulation returned to her arms and hurt 'like the dickens.' according to her muttered complaints.

"Are you done yet?" Madison whispered to her friend.

"No! This is some kind of super knot. It won't budge, and that tin keeps breaking. I can't do this in the dark. We've got to think of something else."

"I think I hear Maury coming back. Granny, can you scoot your way to the doorway? I've got a plan."


Maury moved stealthily through the old power house, but the women were ready for him. Their ears tuned in to the sound of his soft footsteps. They knew when he snapped an unseen twig in two, knew when his toe encountered a loose bolt and sent it skittering across the floor. They heard the rustle of his clothes, and knew he was close.

By the time they heard his breath, labored but measured, he was only inches away.

Granny, her feet still securely bound, sat on the floor on one side of the opening, while Genny squatted low on the other side. As Maury stepped cautiously through the doorway, his eyes scanned the room in front of him, searching the darkened space for his prisoner.

He never saw the rope. On the silent count of three, the women raised the braided strand and pulled it taut. Maury tripped and went down hard.

They counted on the concrete floor to deliver a hard and unforgiving blow. They didn't account for how far the big man would fall, or how wide his sprawl. Maury yelped as he landed on a huge gear with thick, vicious teeth. A nearby pile of gnarled and rusted tin bit into his face.

Madison was ready with her long and heavy pipe. Her swing lost much of its force as she struck him across the shoulders, if for nothing else but good measure. From the sounds of the man's pitiful moans, he was already incapacitated.

"Get his gun!" Genny advised.

"See if he has a knife," Granny Bert prioritized. She wanted free.

Madison found both. While the other two worked to saw through the ropes binding her grandmother's feet, Madison questioned Maury as she held his gun on him.

"Are you the only one here?"

When he only groaned, she nudged him with her foot. "Answer me! Are you the only one out here?"

He muttered yes without moving.

Taking him at his word, Madison used her phone to call Sophie. The moment the innkeeper answered, she heard the commotion in the background. "We have my grandmother," Madison said without preamble. "I hope all that racket means your friend arrived and has the men in custody."

The innkeeper sounded breathless. "Yes, yes. Logan arrived and has everything under control. Is your grandmother all right?"

Genny's flashlight app illuminated the space, giving them their first good look at the older woman. Finally free of the ropes, Granny Bert stomped around to restore blood flow to her feet. Her clothes were ruined, blood dried upon her cheek, her body visibly shook from a mixture of cold and nerves, and there were rope burns around both wrists. Her hair was a mess, matted with dust, rust, pieces of leaves, twigs, and spider webs. To Madison, she'd never looked better.

"She looks great," Madison answered with a smile.

"Send the police out to the old cotton mill, to the abandoned power house ruins. We'll have Maury tied up and waiting for them."


Granny Bert refused medical aid, insisting all she needed was a bed, a stiff drink, and a warm blanket, not necessarily in that order.

Logan McKee introduced herself as a member of a security agency, although she never clearly identified the exact one. After a quick debriefing and whiskey-laced hot toddies, she arranged for the CIA, FBI, Homeland Security, and assorted other officials to return the next day for formal questioning. Cold and exhausted, the women gratefully retired for the night, but sleep was slow to come. After a hot, soaking bath, Granny Bert crawled into bed, tucked securely beneath a warm blanket and two pairs of watchful eyes.

"I'm ready to go home," Genny confessed.

"Maybe we're not cut out to be spies," the older woman agreed. Her voice was muffled beneath the covers piled on top of her. She couldn't seem to shake the chill that had settled into her bones. "I've had enough of all this secret code business."

"I couldn't agree more," Madison said. "I miss my B's." At Genny's questioning look, she clarified, "Bethani, Blake, and Brash."

"Have you called them yet?"

"No," she admitted. "I haven't figured out how to explain it yet."

"Me, either. I texted Cutter and told him I would call later, but I know he'll hear it in my voice."

"It's almost midnight at home. With any luck, they're all asleep and won't realize we didn't call."

# 24

Monitoring a big fire between Naomi and Riverton as it played out over the police scanner, Brash didn't hear the teens when they pulled in the drive. He was in the family room when the front door chimed their arrival.

The team at *Home Again* originally designated the space as the media room. Thanks to the generous sponsors of the show, it came stocked with cutting-edge electronics, state-of-the-art surround sound, and the finest in-home theater furnishings. Second only to the farmhouse-style kitchen, it was everyone's favorite room in the house, but Madison said calling it the *media room* sounded too technical. She renamed it the family room, insisting the term was a better fit.

"In here," Brash called. He started up from the reclining seat, but the trio was already in the room, plus one.

He eyed the girl with the purple streaks in her hair and the dark makeup. "I didn't realize we were having a guest this evening." His tone remained friendly, but his gaze was sharp as he turned to Bethani. "Does your mother object?"

With a heavy and audible sigh, Blake stepped out from behind his sister and lifted his head. "Oh, she'll object to just about everything that happened tonight."

"Blake! What happened to your face? And why do all of you reek of smoke?" Brash ran his sharp blue gaze over the four of them. Concern edged into his infamous imperial smirk. "Singed shoes, smutty pants, dirty hands. Who wants to go first?"

"I will." Megan was quick to volunteer. "Daddy, this is our new friend, Tasha Garrison. Tasha, this is my father, Police Chief Brash deCordova."

The moment they pulled up at the Big House, Tasha recognized the old mansion from the television reality show. With only the briefest of explanations, her new friends admitted to their real identity. Bethani made some excuse about escaping the notoriety and wanting to make friends on her own merit, not her fleeting flame. Tasha had taken the news in stride, even though she still looked a bit dazed. It was hard to know if it stemmed from this new revelation or from the night's events.

Hearing the formal title attached to his name, the dark-haired girl grew noticeably anxious. Bethani threaded her arm through the girl's to control her trembling. "It's okay, Tasha," she said softly. "He's a good guy."

Brash's eyes warmed with the praise from his soon-to-be stepdaughter, but he didn't allow it to distract him. "Hello, Tasha. Bethani told me she made a new friend. It's nice to meet you." He graced the frightened teen with a tolerant smile and a gentle greeting. But as he turned to his daughter, his demeanor hardened. "I'm waiting for an explanation."

"Before we tell you the whole story and you blow up like I know you will, I want you to know that Blake was a true hero tonight. He probably saved my life." Going up on tiptoe, Megan brushed a kiss across the lanky teen's bruised cheek. "Thanks, bro. I owe you one."

"What you owe is an explanation," Brash said, losing his patience. "Let's all have a seat, and then I want to hear the whole sordid story. Tasha, let's start with you. After you call your father, you can tell me how you know my kids."


"Your dad is so cool," Tasha proclaimed the next morning. Wearing one of Megan's light-blue blouses and with her face scrubbed clean, she looked like a completely different person than the one they first met. Even her purple-streaked hair, styled with a bit of curl and Bethani's special touch, looked more trendy than harsh.

After hearing explanations from each of the four teens the night before, Brash delayed passing judgment on their exploits. Instead, he sent them to bed and said they would discuss it over breakfast.

"Yeah, he is pretty awesome," Megan agreed. Her smile turned to a grimace as she added, "Let's just hope we still think so after we hear his verdict."

"We might as well get this over with and go help cook breakfast," Bethani said.

As the girls descended from their third-floor rooms, Tasha was clearly in awe. "I can't believe you two actually live in this house. It's amazing."

"Well, technically, I don't live here yet," Megan corrected. "But even before our parents got engaged, I was over here all the time."

"I can see why. This house is awesome."

"What sounds good for breakfast?" Bethani asked her guest.

Tasha shrugged her shoulders. "I dunno."

"What do you and your dad usually eat?"

"How would I know what he eats? I never see him." Her voice took on a petulant tone.

"Really? That's sad," Megan said. "Not only do I have an awesome dad, I've got an awesome stepfather, and soon I'll have an awesome stepmother. I like spending time with all my parents."

"My dad never has time for me. Sometimes, it's like he forgets I even exist."

Bethani paused on the second-floor landing. "I sorta know what you mean," she admitted. "Before my dad died, he didn't have a lot of time for me and Blake."

"Really?" Megan peered around Tasha to look at her best friend. "I've never heard you say that before. You always talk about how great he was."

"He was." Her voice took on a defensive note, but as she toyed with the intricate carvings on the newel post, the argument escaped on a sigh. "I know I usually blame my mom for their problems, but the truth is, my father had changed those last couple of years. He started missing my recitals. He never had time for Blake's games, or for family game night, or for anything that involved *us*. If it wasn't for work or with his *assistant*"—her voice took on an air of disdain—"he wasn't interested."

Megan rubbed her friend's arm. "I'm sorry, Beth," she murmured. "I never knew."

She lifted a shoulder as if to say it didn't matter, even when they all knew her heart still ached. Turning the attention away from herself, the teen addressed Tasha, "Is that how it is with your dad? Does he have an *assistant*?"

"No. He just works all the time. He even took a second job. Sometimes... sometimes, I think it's so he doesn't have to be stuck at the house with me." Her lip trembled as she made the admission.

"I doubt that's it, Tasha," Megan said encouragingly. "Maybe he just finds the house too lonely without your mom there. Maybe working is how he deals with his grief."

"What about *my* grief?" The girl tossed her head and flounced onto the first step.

"How did your mom die?" Bethani's tone was gentle as they continued down the stairs.

"She had cancer."

"Maybe he has a lot of medical bills," the blond suggested. "My mom tries not to let it show, but I know she worries a lot about money. She's taken on some crazy jobs, just to pay the bills."

"Maybe," Tasha said, a groove of consideration between her brows. "But if that's the case, I could get a job. I could make enough to cover my own spending money."

"Parents are funny like that," Megan chipped in. "They don't want to worry us, so they pretend everything's okay and make things harder on themselves."

"And in the long run, it ends up affecting us anyway," Bethani agreed. She took a sniff of the air. "Mmm. Smells like Mr. de already started breakfast."

Brash and Blake were already at work when the girls walked into the kitchen. Blake broke eggs into a large mixing bowl, while Brash dipped thick slices of bread into a concoction in the smaller bowl. Notes of cinnamon, vanilla, and coffee floated on the air.

"Smells delish in here!" Megan announced.

Blake looked up from his task, his eyes immediately seeking out Tasha. When he saw her without her dark makeup and her usual uninspired clothes, he almost dropped the egg he held.

Bethani sashayed up beside her twin and whispered so that no one else could hear, "I like my eggs without drool, thank you very much. Pull it together, twin." She bumped him in the arm and went on to the refrigerator, where she retrieved the container of orange juice.

"Good morning, ladies. Sleep well?" Brash asked in his warm baritone.

"Morning," Megan said, brushing her father's cheek with a kiss. "Slept great. Would've still been snoozing, if you hadn't sent me that text." She narrowed her eyes in playful accusation.

"I figured as much. Why don't you and Tasha set the table? There's seven of us."

"Mom's already home?" Bethani asked in surprise, her eyes flying toward the door.

"Not yet. Cutter is joining us for breakfast."

Tasha's eyes went wide. "Cutter Montgomery, the hot fireman?" Blake didn't miss the note of awe that slipped into her voice.

Ignoring the girl's dazed reaction, Megan did a visual count of the room. "That's only one more. That makes six."

Brash expertly flipped a slice of French toast. His voice sounded casual as he said, "I invited Tasha's dad to join us."

The dark-haired girl had been exchanging shy glances with Blake, but she stiffened at the news. "He works on Saturdays," she said.

"He took off to join us."

"He did?" From her tone, it was obvious she didn't know whether to be flattered or frightened. Her father seldom took a day off work, least of all for her. How angry would he be when he arrived?

"Sure did. I've known your father for several years. I was sorry to see him step down as a road commissioner, but I admired how he put his daughter before his career. He's a man after my own heart."

Brash sent his daughter a warm smile before sneaking a peek at the purple-haired girl. Her brow puckered in confusion, as if she had considered the possibility for the first time.

With a tiny smile of satisfaction, the policeman turned back to his toast making.

# 25

Early on Saturday morning, the alphabet agencies converged upon *The Columbia Inn at Peralynna* to take depositions and statements from all three women. The flight back to Texas was re-scheduled for the afternoon, leaving time for a leisurely lunch once the interrogations were finished.

To ensure complete privacy, the entire meeting took place in their penthouse suite. By then, it was clear Logan McKee was not only part of the CIA, but the officer in charge of the entire mission.

She stayed behind to visit and to offer bits and pieces of unclassified information from the case. "I'm sorry I'm not at liberty to tell you more but trust me when I say you ladies did a huge service for our country." The officer dipped her blond head in a gesture of thanks.

"So Beady Eyes/Black Jacket was really an agent, as well?" Madison confirmed, trying to solidify the fact in her mind. That particular scenario never occurred to her.

The other woman laughed. "I've never heard that code name before, but yes, Officer Marino is one of our best."

Granny Bert fell short of hiding her snort. "If he's

so all-fired good, why did he mistake us for the other side?"

"An innocent mistake, I can assure you." The case officer raised her hand as if taking an oath. "Under the circumstances, anyone could have misinterpreted the situation. Officer Marino witnessed you, Madison, intercept the note intended for one of our people. He thought you could be the rogue double agent known only as Kalypso. No one knows exactly what she looks like, given that she's a master of disguises. His suspicion seemed confirmed when you checked in here at *Peralynna*, the very place another important exchange was to happen. When you and your grandmother visited the Cryptology Museum… he was certain you were counter intelligence, trying to decode the Lilac Code for your own purposes."

"The Lilac Code?" Madison echoed.

Logan McKee inclined her blond head. "The code name associated with this operation."

"I still don't understand how they mistook three of us for one agent," Genny pitched in.

"If I understood correctly, you and Madison were the only ones present when the child approached you."

"That's right," Madison remembered, tapping her grandmother's hand. "You had gone to the restroom."

Logan shrugged a lean shoulder. "Obukov was instructed to meet our person in your exact location. The truth is," she paused for a moment, deciding how much of the truth to divulge, "our officer posed as the mysterious Kalypso. And where Kalypso is concerned, two or more people could be a plausible disguise. Unfortunately, our officer was detained, and Obukov mistook you for the wrong person."

Genny picked up on the name. "Who's Obukov?"

"The man you knew as Barton."

"Obukov? What kind of name is that?" Granny Bert wanted to know. "Does he work for the Russians?"

"I'm afraid I'm not at liberty to say."

"I'm still confused," confessed Madison. "Beady Eyes—Marino—was the one who took my suitcase by mistake? Then stole his case back from my room?"

"Not exactly. The case belonged to another agent-for-hire named Murdock. Murray, as you knew him. Officer Marino was merely on the flight for surveillance, to ensure we weren't double-crossed. Apparently, he took his eyes off the case for only a moment. There was a disturbance involving a child—"

"Yes," Madison murmured, recalling the ruckus near his row. "A toddler had a meltdown and caused a bit of a scene."

"During the confusion, apparently no one noticed when your suitcase was placed in front of the other one. Murdoch took yours by mistake, leaving you with his. Which left him with a major problem, since he was meeting the buyer for his case—myself—here at the hotel."

"So, he really did steal it, then."

"Oh, no. The hotel has excellent security," Logan McKee assured them. "Please understand, no one else can find, nor use, the hidden staircase. But after much discussion, the agency determined that for the safety of the three of you, it was best we intervened. Please forgive us, but in the name of national security, Officer Marino and I accessed your room through the secret passageway and retrieved the case."

"If you're the one who took it, why did Maury kidnap me?" Granny Bert demanded. "And why did a scoundrel like that bother giving Maddy her luggage back?"

"Again, that was us," the operations officer

BECKI WILLIS

explained. "We returned your abandoned suitcase as soon as we found it. As for Murdoch, he was desperate to salvage something from the botched operation. He had lost the codebooks; Obukov had lost the message they deciphered. The two teamed up to steal them back and sell one, or both, to the highest bidder."

"That's what those were? Codebooks?" Madison asked in surprise. "But—"

This time when Logan raised her palm, it signified a dead end. "Please. I've revealed as much as I can. Suffice it to say, the message held very sensitive information. Having the codebooks in our possession saves hours of work, but even so, our people have been up all night, deciphering the details. We've learned some of our enemy's plans. Once we have all the clues, we can establish a timeline and the order of certain events. We may quite possibly avert a national crisis."

Genny nudged her friend. "Maddy already knows the order. Go on. Tell her how you cracked the code."

The officer looked slightly amused. Definitely skeptical. "*You* cracked the Lilac Code?"

With a scowl, Madison shook her head. "No, of course not. I have no idea what the actual message said. I was simply playing around with how it might be read." She waved away her own foolishness. "I'm sure your experts saw the same thing I did."

"Oh?" The casual note in Officer McKee's voice belied the eagerness in her green eyes. "Tell me more."

Madison explained her theory. She used a pen and paper to illustrate the loops and their specific order, as she imagined them. When Maddy finished her demonstration, the officer looked astounded.

"I can't believe it," she murmured, momentarily at a loss for words.

Her stunned expression was fleeting. With a sharp intake of breath, the woman transformed before their eyes. One moment, Logan McKee was a smiling, polite conversationalist; the next moment, she was a highly trained federal agent, ready for action. With subtle economy of motion, her spine straightened, her shoulders squared, and her green eyes glittered with anticipation. She reminded Madison of a snake, coiling for a strike. Energy radiated from her.

"Ladies, it has been a pleasure. You have my contact information, should you ever need to reach me. Please accept these small gifts as a token of my appreciation." She slid an envelope toward each of them, but she had already taken a step back, ready to spring into action. "I'm sorry to rush off, but duty calls."

With that, the blond officer fairly bounded from the suite, her phone already to her ear.

"What in the world..."

"I think you were right," Granny Bert smirked. "I think you just outsmarted all their fancy experts, and she can't wait to test your theory."

"Maybe." Madison's tone didn't sound very confident. She reached for her envelope and slid a nail beneath the seal. "I wonder what these are."

Genny was the first to reply, her voice filled with excitement. "I don't know about yours, but mine is a gift certificate for an extended weekend here at *Peralynna*. In Suite C, no less, their most luxurious and romantic suite! Plus, a couple's massage." Her blue eyes twinkled as her dimples deepened. "The perfect honeymoon, don't you think?"

Holding up an identical certificate, Madison agreed, her own eyes mirroring the twinkle.

"Mine's better than both yours combined," Granny Bert gloated, waving her envelope in the air. "A certain celebrity chef will be preparing a private meal, just for me. In one of Austin's swankiest hotels."

As they each tucked their coveted certificates away for safe keeping, Madison checked her watch. "Time to head for the airport, girls."

After the previous evening's events, Granny Bert was a bit slow getting to her feet, but her smile was as lively as ever. "Well, Genny girl, we promised you a trip you'd never forget. I'd say we lived up to that promise, wouldn't you?"

Genny laughed aloud. "And then some! Come on, girls. Let's go home!"

# 26

"You're sure you won't go home with us?" Madison asked for a final time.

"Girl, I'm all tuckered out." Granny Bert made a shooing motion with her hand as they stood on her doorstep. "I have to unpack this suitcase, wash clothes, and bake a sheet cake for Genny's church shower tomorrow. You two run along so I can get to bed sometime before midnight."

"With all that's happened, I completely forgot about my shower!" Genny cried, aghast at her own thoughtlessness.

Not so long ago, the community had given her a 'fire shower' after her house burned down. Genny felt guilty about having another shower so soon, particularly when tomorrow's wasn't the only one. Two weeks ago, friends of the Montgomery family hosted a huge shower honoring the couple and last weekend, employees at *New Beginnings* had surprised them with a come and go shower at the café. Customers dropped in throughout the day to offer best wishes and donations for the money tree. Overwhelmed with such generosity and the outpouring of gifts and support, Genny almost felt bad about tomorrow's shower at church, and her lingerie shower yet to come.

"Go on, now. Go see that man of yours," Granny Bert said, giving her arm a gentle push. "You, too, Maddy. Give the kids a hug for me and tell them I'll see 'em tomorrow."

Five minutes later, Madison and Genny pulled into the driveway of the old mansion. It wasn't nearly as large or stately as the Maryland mansion they just came from, but it was every bit as beautiful. Once a cold and formal affair, the house was now warm and inviting. It was no longer simply a house. It was now a *home*.

Cutter and Brash stood outside, awaiting their arrival.

"That's a sight I look forward to!" Genny beamed. "Cutter, waiting for me to come home each day."

Madison laughed at her friend's eager descent from the car. "At least wait until I put it in park!" she playfully grumbled.

While Cutter whooped and swung his fiancé around in his arms, laughing and showering her with kisses, Brash had a more subtle greeting for his would-be bride. He held the door for her as she slid from behind the wheel, but there was a heated simmer in his eyes as he pulled her into his arms.

"Welcome home, sweetheart." His deep voice rumbled against her as he held her close, savoring a moment of nearness before dipping his mouth to hers.

"I missed you," Madison murmured against his lips.

"I missed you, too. Let's not do this again."

Madison pulled back in surprise. Did he already know about their adventure in Maryland? Both she and Genny had been deliberately vague on the phone, choosing to tell them the story in person. Brash, however, was law enforcement. It would be like him to already know of her unexpected exploits with the alphabet community.

"Do what?" she asked, keeping her voice as innocent as possible.

When he cupped the back of her head with his hand and pulled her in for another kiss, she realized he wasn't referring to the secret codes and Granny Bert's kidnapping. His blue eyes held a different meaning altogether. "Let's not spend four days apart, ever again."

"It's been a long four days," she agreed. *In more ways than you know.* She raised her smiling face to his. "How did you make it with three teenagers in the house? Are they inside? I can't wait to see them!"

"We've been busy," Brash acknowledged.

Something in his guarded expression made her frown. Her mother's intuition kicked in. "What aren't you telling me?"

"Let's get your suitcases out. The girls have dinner ready."

"Bethani and Megan cooked?" Madison's eyes narrowed in suspicion. "What did they do? I don't know about Megan, but Bethani only cooks when she's trying to finagle her way out of being grounded."

Brash smoothly avoided a direct answer. "Maybe she's just being thoughtful. Did you ever think of that? Maybe she knows you've been traveling all day and would appreciate a hot, home-cooked meal. It may not look like it, but they've been working on it all afternoon." He chuckled, thinking of the disaster he had walked into earlier. He helped clean up the kitchen and get it into a semblance of order.

"What did they make?"

"My mom gave them the recipe to my favorite dish, King Ranch Chicken."

"Mmm," Madison said with approval. "I love her recipe."

"Just remember," he cautioned. "Sometimes things are fine, even though they don't always look so pretty."


"Blake! What happened to your face?" Madison cried in alarm, the moment she saw her son. She tugged at his chin, turning his face for closer scrutiny. "Did you get into a *fight*?" The thought was preposterous, but his black eye and bruises suggested otherwise.

She whirled toward Brash. "Is this what you wouldn't tell me? Is this what doesn't always look so pretty?" Her fiery eyes flashed to her daughter next. "What's your part in this? You don't cook for no reason, so I know this involves you, too." She turned back to her son, whose chin she still held. "Well?" she demanded. "Aren't you going to explain? And are you all right?"

With a slight wince, Blake pulled free of her grasp. "Thanks for finally asking," he said dryly. "And I'm fine. Can we talk about this over dinner? I'm starving."

"Don't think you're getting out of a full explanation, young man."

"I'm not trying to. I'll tell you every sordid detail." Flashing one of his charming smiles, he added, "Just as soon as I have the strength to talk."

"What's it been since you last ate?" his sister sneered. "Thirty minutes?"

The snark in her words skimmed over his head. "See what I mean? My stomach's starting to cave in!"

Megan shoved a bowl into his hands. "Here, take this salad to the table. I'll pour the tea and we can eat." She brushed against Madison and kissed her cheek. "Welcome home, Momma Maddy."

Promptly losing her starch, Madison apologized with a weary sigh. "I'm sorry," she said, ruffling Megan's auburn hair. "I didn't even say hello. I saw Blake's eye and panicked." Madison made the rounds, hugging and kissing all three teenagers with genuine affection. "I missed all of you, you know."

"We missed you, too, Mom," Bethani said, busy taking the casserole from the oven. "Someone call Aunt Genny and Cutter. Grandma Lydia gave me her recipe and I don't want dinner getting cold."

The authoritative words sounded so foreign coming from the teenager's mouth. Madison stood back in amazement, watching as the teenagers hustled about the kitchen, working in sync. Blake carried the steaming dish to the table, while Megan poured iced tea and Bethani scooped corn into a serving bowl. The table was already set and even had a candle arrangement as a centerpiece.

"I'm leaving you in charge more often!" Madison whispered to Brash, clearly impressed.

His arm snaked around her waist. "Nuh-uh," he objected. "Remember? You aren't leaving again, not without me."

"Which reminds me. I found the perfect place for our honeymoon."

He brushed his question against her ear. "Does it have a bed?"

Fighting off a blush, Madison nodded. "Yes."

"Then it sounds perfect." Scorched by his heated purr and the possessive hand low on her hip, Madison could no longer control the color slipping into her cheeks. They both knew it would be a long six weeks until their honeymoon took place.

Nudging him in the ribs, Madison muttered

something about behaving himself as she turned her attention back to the scene in her kitchen. As alien as it seemed, her babies had the meal under control without any help from her.

It hit her hard, right in her solar plexus.

Her babies were no longer babies. They were growing into fine, responsible young adults, a fact that was reiterated when she heard of their recent brush with danger.

They were gathered now in the family room, discussing the matter that sprawled well beyond the dining room table. Bethani curled at Madison's feet as her mother absently ran her fingers through the long, blond tresses. Blake sat to his mother's right, still within her reach. She touched his knee often, as if to reassure herself that he was fine.

"What were you thinking?" she chided softly. Her voice was filled more with worry than with ire. "You could have been seriously injured."

"The jerks deserved to lose their cars, but I couldn't just let them blow up, Mom. We could have all been hurt."

His mother continued to fret. "But you came so close. Your jeans were seared."

"Not to mention my boots are now toast."

"I'll buy you a new pair," Cutter offered. "Compliments of the fire department." He shot Madison an apologetic look. "I know it was a close call, but Blake thought fast on his feet and avoided a potential disaster. He did the right thing. He put out the smaller fire and called in backup for the big one. I know a lot of grown men who wouldn't have been as proactive as he was."

"I'm proud of you, honey, for what you did." Madison hugged her son, who squirmed uncomfortably under all the praise. He was unprepared for the follow-up, when his mother bopped him in the chest. "But don't ever do something that dangerous again!" she admonished.

Rubbing the spot on his chest, he looked a bit sheepish. "Yes, ma'am."

"I'm serious! What possessed you three—" she encompassed the girls with her fiery glare, "to follow a group of kids you barely know out to an abandoned warehouse?"

"They said we were having a bonfire," Bethani defended their actions. "We thought they had permission to be there."

"Brash and I gave you permission to go to the *Dairy Queen*. When you left there, did you tell Brash the location had changed?"

The teen dropped her blue yes. "No, ma'am."

"Is that the way to build trust? To tell us you're going one place, and then sneak off and go to another?"

"No, ma'am."

"We weren't sneaking," Blake said, a touch of defiance slipping into his words. "And as soon as we realized what was going on, we tried to leave."

"But you knew you shouldn't have been there in the first place, correct?"

His mother's piercing gaze was intense. He dropped his eyes. "Yes, ma'am."

Madison paused, forcing herself to pull in a deep breath before releasing it slowly. "Who were these kids, anyway?"

"A bunch of creeps. No wonder Tasha's dad was worried. She shouldn't have ever been hanging out with them in the first place." The words rang of proprietary protection, a sound not lost upon his mother. She would have to ask more about this Tasha girl, but Blake's love life could wait. His safety couldn't.

"Brash?" she asked, turning toward him. "Who are these kids?"

"It would be easy to say they're a bunch of thugs," the law officer admitted, heaving a sigh, "but that's not entirely right. Most of them are what the system calls 'troubled.' They come from broken homes and dysfunctional families. They've had brushes with the law, but instead of getting the help they need, they've gotten pushed aside and forgotten. A couple of them aren't bad kids, just bored and easily influenced. They've fallen in with the wrong crowd, like Tasha was doing. Easy game for kids like Julio, their so-called 'leader,' who needs the attention. He never gets any at home, so he finds it elsewhere."

"Let me guess. Broken home, left to fend for himself."

"That would be the second-in-charge, Freddie Beach. He spent his childhood shuffled from one relative or one foster home to another. Julio actually comes from a steady, if not crowded, home. His father is a hard worker, holding down three jobs to keep their family afloat. There are five or six kids, including a younger brother with serious health problems and a sister with a rough reputation. She's been in and out of detention and drug rehab for the past three years but until about a year ago, Julio never caused any trouble."

"And you know what they say," Cutter murmured. "The squeaky wheel gets the oil."

"What does that mean?" Bethani asked in confusion.

"It means no one paid Julio any attention, until he started causing trouble," her mother said. "Is he still in school?"

"His mother says yes, his teachers say no. Most

days, he skips classes. When he does go, he's usually sent to the principal's office or AE."

"AE?" Genny questioned.

"Alternative Education. The school says he's a distraction and bad influence to the other students. He's been caught smoking and setting small fires around campus, more than once."

"Did they send him to the school counselor?"

"Like that does any good," Blake muttered.

"I hate to say it, but he's right," Cutter put in. "Few school counselors are equipped to deal with these sorts of emotional problems."

"So, they just ignore his cries for help?" Genny frowned. "The boy was setting fires, and no one thought it might lead to something bigger?"

"Turns out he's become quite the fire bug," Cutter continued. "One of the boys admitted setting fire to a couple of abandoned houses. Said it was a service to the community, burning down the eye sores. He may or may not have a point, but unfortunately, it didn't stop there. They moved on to bigger things, and each time, they perfected their skills and added new recruits."

"I don't know about the other times, but I'm pretty sure they used explosives last night," Blake said.

Madison paled as she put a hand to her chest and squeaked, "Explosives?"

"There's this guy named Smokes. He hollered 'fire in the hole,' and then there was this huge boom, and the sky lit up like it was on fire." He used his hands to demonstrate the blast.

"And when Julio said something about timing it, he distinctly called it a charge," Megan recalled.

"What were they timing?" Genny asked.

Cutter drew in a sharp breath and looked at Brash. "We've got to find those kids. There's no doubt in my mind what they're planning next."

"Wait. Those kids aren't in custody?" Madison gasped. "They're still running around, free to set something else on fire?"

"Three of them—one girl and two boys—were located and brought in for questioning, but they refuse to cooperate. One admitted to burning down the empty houses in Riverton and one hinted at something big in the works, but that's all they're saying."

Brash added what little he could. "There's a warrant out for the one they call Smokes. He's the only one of legal age. His father has a military background in explosives, and apparently, the kid picked up a few tricks of his own."

"How many others are there?" Madison asked. Her forehead creased in a frown.

"Five are unaccounted for. The three main firebugs, Smokes, Julio, and Freddie, plus another girl, and a boy they call Django. No one knows his real name."

Megan nodded. "He was the one with the timer."

"I still don't understand the point of the timer," Bethani admitted.

Genny turned toward her fiancé. "You said you know what they're planning next. What *is* next?"

Cutter's worried gaze met Brash's, darting briefly to the teenagers in the room. With a slight nod of his head, the lawman gave his approval to continue.

"This is to go no further than this room," he cautioned. "Blake, Bethani, Megan, you can't share this with your friends. Not even with Tasha. Understood?"

After all three teens pledged their silence, the fire chief continued, "Again, this stays between us. We don't want to cause widespread panic, or to tip our hand with Julio by letting him know we're on to him. I've been studying the fires and I see a pattern of progression. I shared my concerns with law enforcement, and they're in agreement. Given the fact most of the kids involved are juvenile delinquents who have either dropped out of school or who have a history of problems with teachers and other figures of authority, I have no doubt their ultimate target is a school."

"They're going to burn down a school? That's sick!" Blake proclaimed.

Madison stood from the couch and paced the room, rubbing her arms to ward off the sudden chill she felt. "I can see that," she murmured. "Julio feels left out at home, however unintentional that may be. His parents' attention is stretched thin, focused on the sick brother and the troubled sister, not to mention several other siblings. He turned to the school for help, hoping to draw their attention by setting small fires, but no one recognized his cry for help. Instead, he was ostracized and sent to AE for even more isolation. He feels angry and betrayed, so now he's lashing out."

"Are you a shrink or something?" Megan asked, clearly impressed by her assessment.

"I minored in Psychology. For a while, I considered becoming a counselor."

"You're good. And that makes total sense." Megan bobbed her head. "A school should be a place to find help and support. It shouldn't be a place to be bullied, or where you're labeled a distraction and beyond help. It should be a safe place, physically *and* emotionally. I can see where Julio thinks it let him down."

"Let's be clear. Normal, healthy minds don't automatically seek revenge," Madison pointed out. "Betrayed or not, most people don't retaliate, particularly on such a drastic level."

"I think this boy has more emotional problems than anyone realized," Brash stated, his tone ominous.

Blake's forehead puckered as he considered his words. "You think he'll become another school shooter?" he asked worriedly.

"When you're as troubled as these boys, the issue isn't which weapon they'll choose. They could use a gun, a car driven into a crowd, or a bomb. Or fire. According to Cutter, Julio set an office on fire, knowing there were people inside."

Bethani's face lost all color. "You mean... he's going to set the school on fire with people inside? Is that what the timer is for, to see how long they're trapped inside?"

"It's a very real possibility."

The teen clutched her stomach. "I feel sick. We— We actually hung out with the creep!"

Megan flew to her feet. "He *liked* me! He tried coming on to me!" She shimmied her shoulders and stomped her feet, as if to throw off his unwanted attention. "I feel dirty. Smutty." It seemed a more appropriate word.

"And Freddie tried to hook up with *me*," Bethani yelped. "He even has my phone number." She grabbed her phone and scrolled through her contacts.

"Wait. You have his number?" Brash asked sharply.

"Only until I can hit delete," the teen assured him.

"Don't. Can I have that number? Maybe we can trace his phone and find his whereabouts."

"Here. Take it. I don't want it. Erase it when you're done." She shivered in revulsion. "Crying out for attention is one thing. But trying to kill innocent people is a whole different thing."

# 27

Valentine's Day dawned clear and cold. It was the perfect day for a wedding.

With Valentine's falling in the middle of the week, for much of the town, it was business as usual. *New Beginnings,* of course, was closed, but schools and most other businesses were in session.

Bethani and Megan begged to stay home, but their parents insisted they go to class. The swaying argument was simple: the girls didn't want to miss the assembly that afternoon. As a fundraiser, the Student Council was selling Val-o-Grams and candy and were crowning a Valentine Queen and King before the entire student body.

If Madison could manage it, she planned to swing by school and attend, but it wasn't looking favorable. Her to-do list was longer than the hours in the day.

She and Genny scuttled between the house and church, swamped with last minute details. The church looked magnificent, adorned with white tulle intertwined with green ivy and red roses. Cutter's sister and sisters-in-law helped decorate, while Granny Bert, Cutter's mother, and a few friends pitched in to prepare the Big House for the reception. It, too, was filled with tulle and flowers.

One of Genny's friends flew in from Boston to make her wedding cake. She worried the elaborate five-tier affair was too fancy for Cutter's taste, but her friend was a celebrated pastry chef with an impressive resume. If he wanted to create something magnificent and give it to her on her wedding day, she wasn't about to refuse. Genny herself made the groom's cake, a decadent chocolate creation shaped as a fireman's helmet. As a special treat, she was surprising her groom with his favorite apple turnovers.

Just before two, Madison texted Blake to tell him she was running late for the assembly.

The teen was on his way from the gym to the auditorium. He read his mother's message, sent her a thumb's up emoji, and stuffed his phone back into his pocket.

A reflection in the distance caught his eye. A chain-link fence separated the school property from a dense grove of trees. In the spring, the trees were green and lush, but in the dead of winter, their limbs were bare and their underbrush sparse. Anything out of place was easily visible.

He immediately noticed the out of place movement among the trees.

Blake stiffened. He couldn't be certain, but he thought he recognized Freddie and Django, hiding behind the spindly trunks.

"Hey, man, I'll catch up with you in a few," Blake told the friend walking with him.

"You sure? You don't wanna be late. You know you probably have like a dozen Val-o-Grams coming."

"I doubt it," Blake snorted.

"Are you kidding? Danni Jo, Kaci, Latricia. You'll probably be crowned King, if they have any say in the matter."

"I'll be there. I just have to run back in the gym."
He turned away before his friend could protest
further.

Blake pretended to head back to the gym, but he
slipped around the side of the building, heading
toward the dumpsters. From there, he had a better
view of the trees.

Not only was that Freddie and Django, but Nae
Nae was there with them. And if they were there, he
had no doubt that Smokes and Julio were somewhere
nearby.

So far, the five had managed to avoid the
authorities. Brash had no luck tracking Freddie's
phone, and their families claimed the teens hadn't
been home since the incident at the oilfield.

Blake knew their presence there today could mean
only one thing. They were targeting the school. *His*
school.

He dialed Cutter's number, grumbling when it
went straight to voicemail. He knew it was his
wedding day, but this was urgent! He called Brash
next, who was in a meeting and couldn't be disturbed.
Frustrated, Blake sent a quick text to both men,
alerting them to Julio and company's presence.

He glanced up to keep an eye on the trio in the
trees but didn't see them. Panicked, Blake moved
along, searching for a better vantage spot. He finally
caught a glimpse of Nae Nae's arm, and the binoculars
she held in her hands.

Blake followed her line of sight, and his blood
turned cold.

With a sick twist of his stomach, Blake knew what
the derelict teens intended. The entire school was
gathering in the auditorium, where they would be
trapped and helpless if a fire broke out.

He paused long enough to text his sister.
***Julio here. Get out. Now!***
As he ran to toward the auditorium, Blake called 911. His words were rushed. "This is Blake Reynolds. I'm at The Sisters High School and I think someone intends to set it on fire. I can't reach Brash deCordova and Cutter Montgomery, but both know the situation and can give you more details. Send help out here now. I'll try to clear the auditorium."

"Sir," the dispatcher responded in cool professionalism, "I need more information. Please tell—"

"Send someone, now!" Blake barked. "People will be trapped in the auditorium. We need firetrucks and police."

"Is this a threat, Mr. Reynolds? Are you—"

Blake's young voice was strong and authoritative. "Just do it!" He stuffed the phone in his pocket as he rounded the corner and raced up the steps to the school's main entrance. In his haste, he stumbled and went down hard, banging his knee on the concrete. He hung onto the handrail and jerked himself back up, hardly missing a beat.

He jerked on the door and found it locked. Growling in frustration, Blake ran to the next entrance. Surely, with parents invited to attend the assembly, the doors closest to the auditorium would be open. But those doors were locked. So were the next ones he tried. Blake banged on each one with both fists, trying to get someone's attention, but a glance through the glass told him the hallways were empty. Everyone was already inside the auditorium.

He pulled out his phone and tried his sister. The call went to voicemail, but he left a quick message. He repeated the process with Megan and his best friend Jamal. Nobody answered.

By the time he tried Brash again, still to no avail, Blake was already at the side entrance of the school. He knew the door was normally left unlocked, for easy flow to and from the athletics department. Finding it locked, Blake knew Julio was responsible. Somehow, the boy had managed to seal all the entrances and trap everyone inside.

He looked around for something to smash through the glass. There wasn't as much as a twig nearby, much less a limb. Spotting a trash can down the sidewalk, he hoped it would work. He dumped the plastic lid and half-filled liner onto the grass, muttering an apology to the school janitors. The drum was made of heavy steel, which he awkwardly wrestled up the inclining sidewalk. Back at the doors, Blake hefted the bulky cylinder over his head. The weight almost toppled him backwards. He regained his balance and heaved the can with all his might.

The drum hit the thick glass with a loud thud, bounced off, and smacked the teen directly in the chest. Blake was knocked to the ground, momentarily stunned. The tempered glass remained unfazed.

Shaking off the shock, Blake knew he had to try something else. He hoped to have better luck with a classroom window. He raced back down the sidewalk, his eyes searching for the best way in.

He saw movement out of the corner of his eye, but he only had a glimpse of a leg before it disappeared. He thought he recognized the heavy army boot as the kind Julio and Smokes wore. He would have given chase, but something more important demanded his attention.

There was no mistaking the small stack of dynamite placed at the base of the auditorium's back wall.

With a quick about-face, Blake ran back the way he

came, grabbed the heavy trash can, and hauled it with him. Working as quickly as his trembling hands and knocking knees allowed, he turned the drum upside down and set it over the dynamite. With any luck, it would take the brunt of the blast and dull its impact.

His phone rang as he hurried away from the site.

"Blake! What's going on?" his sister demanded.

"Julio and his friends are here. They've set at least one blast. You have to get out of there, Beth."

"Where are you?"

"Side door, toward the football field. All the doors are locked. I can't get in."

"You don't need in!"

"I've gotta warn the others."

"I'll do it," his sister said stubbornly.

"No. Set off the fire alarm by the front doors of the auditorium. Then get out."

"I'm already headed your way."

Blake reached the door as his sister raced into the far end of the hall. She was quite the sight. She held a vase of red roses in one hand, with two heart-shaped boxes of candy snuggled into the crook of her arm. None of it slowed her down in the least. Blond streamers flew behind her, her hair wild, as her long legs closed the distance. "That girl should be in track," he murmured in appreciation.

"I see you!" his sister said needlessly, her breath labored from the race through the hallways.

"See if you can open the door." He knew it was no use, but he rattled the handle from the outside anyway.

Bethani's eyes suddenly widened in horror and she screeched, "Blake! Behind you! Watch out!"

He turned in time to see Julio behind him, but not in time to avoid his attack. Without warning, the angry teen head-butted Blake with staggering force.

The unexpected blow sent him to his knees. As he slung the hair and the shooting stars from his eyes, he struggled back to his feet.

"You sorry, back-stabbing, pansy-assed piece of trash!" Julio flung the words at him, spittle and fire flying from his mouth. He added several colorful insults, but Blake barely heard them. Still stunned from the blow to his forehead, Blake had trouble focusing. "I trusted you, man! I brought you into the fold. But you were setting me up, weren't you? Playing me for a fool!" He popped Blake in the face with his balled fist, sending him into a backwards sprawl on the sidewalk.

His face swam before Blake's blurred eyes.

"You tricked me. Your old man is the heat!" Julio accused. "You brought this on, man. You brought this war to your turf. You'll learn that anyone who messes with me is gonna get burned!" He emphasized the threat with a kick to Blake's ribs.

Regaining his reflexes, Blake grabbed the boy's ankle and gave it a hard twist. Julio fell to the sidewalk with a thud and a curse. Still dizzy, Blake managed to get to his feet, seconds before the other boy.

They faced off, their fists raised. It was the age-old dance of the fight. One moved this way, the other followed. One advanced, the other retreated, only to turn the tables and make the next advance. They circled round and round, sizing up their opponent, waiting for the right moment to strike. Julio got off the first jab, but Blake ducked away in time. He came up with a pop to the other boy's chin.

Bethani pushed through the door, ready to come to her brother's defense. Neither boy noticed her as they got off a half-dozen good punches each. She hung back, waiting for a chance to wade in without being struck by their thrashing fists. But when Julio backed Blake against the railing and delivered consecutive blows to his stomach, she knew she had to act.

Bethani lifted the roses high above her head, stood behind Julio, and brought the glass vase down with all her strength. It cracked over the boy's head, broke into a dozen pieces, and fell with Julio as he hit the ground.

She peered down at his inert form crumpled on the sidewalk, covered now with water, greenery, and the battered petals of her Valentine's Day roses. "I didn't *kill* him, did I?" she whispered, her face pale.

Blake shook his head, not yet able to speak.

Satisfied she had done no fatal harm, Bethani quickly removed her belt. "Help me with his hands," she told her brother. "We'll tie him to the rails."

Wincing, Blake bent to hold the unconscious boy's hands on either side of a metal rail. Bethani made quick work of binding his hands together with her pink sparkly belt.

"Hurry," Blake pressed.

"I can finish here. You go on. The door's open now."

"You sure? What if he comes to?"

"I got this," his sister assured him. She was already busy tying his boot laces together, looping them through the railings, as well. Julio wasn't getting free, anytime soon. Not without help.

"You stay here. I'll clear the auditorium," Blake said.

"Don't cause a panic," his sister called after him. "And don't play the hero. Be safe, twin."

"You, too, twin."

Blake caught sight of himself in the door's reflection. The sight of him, alone, would stir widespread fear. He took a few seconds to slick down his hair, wipe the blood from his lip, and straighten his shirt. Then he was off to a run, praying he wasn't too late.

The doors to the auditorium were locked from the outside. Just as he suspected, Julio had the students and most of the teachers unwittingly trapped inside. Working against time and the knot in his stomach, Blake raced around to all three entrances, unlocking and clearing the doorways.

He burst into the auditorium, just as the president of the student council announced this year's king.

"By popular vote, we have selected this year's Valentines' Day King as... Blake Reynolds! Here he is now, in fact! Blake, come on up to the stage." The girl faltered as she saw his disheveled appearance. "Um, somebody must have just crawled out of bed in time for the presentation," she chided, her tone only half-teasing. "From the looks of it, I'd say you weren't expecting to win. I assume you don't have an acceptance speech ready?"

Despite his busted lip, Blake pasted on a huge smile and bounded onto the stage. "You're right, Heather. I don't have my speech ready," he said into the microphone. "That's because I've been working on a surprise of my own. Everyone needs to follow me outside, right now. You aren't going to believe this!" He used exaggerated arm movements to motion the student body off their seats and toward the doors. A murmur went through the crowd as they slowly rose to their feet. "No pushing, no shoving, but you've got to hurry to see it!" he encouraged them. He saw the principal start forward, his face marred with a frown. "I promise, Mr. Mendoza, it's worth it. Just wait until you see what's outside!"

Blake continued with his rally to move the crowd outdoors. "Half of you go out the front door, the other half go out the back. Hurry, so you don't miss it."

"Blake Reynolds, what is the meaning of this?" the club sponsor demanded. She stepped from the corner of the stage to confront him. Down on the floor, the principal called for the students to return to their seats and settle down.

Blake covered the microphone with his hand and turned so that no one could read his lips. "I promise, Mrs. Cooley, it's urgent. I'll explain later."

"You can't just barge in here and—"

His voice quiet but steady, Blake looked the teacher in the eye. "There's a bomb. We have to clear the auditorium without causing panic."

To her credit, the teacher remained calm. Her face paled and her eyes widened, but she gulped down a nervous breath and stepped up to the mic. "Mr. Mendoza, if you'll indulge us this once, I take full responsibility." She shot her boss a silent plea with her eyes, before turning her attention to the confused crowd. "Students." Her voice came out warbled, so she tried again. "Minions." Her voice strengthened with a theatrical quality. "Do as your Valentines' Day King commands, else you find yourself thrown in the gallows. Believe me, you'll much prefer the outdoors to the dungeon. Hurry, now, and do his bidding!"

The principal's face turned an angry red as the teacher openly encouraged the students to disregard his authority. He pointed a finger at Blake and shouted something that was lost in the rustle of the crowd. Thinking this was a Valentine's Day gimmick, the students were excited, hurrying to file out the door. They did so with minimum fuss and confusion.

Blake jumped from the stage and faced the principal's angry tirade.

"What is the meaning of this, young man?" he demanded. "You are on the verge of being expelled for—"

"That's fine, Mr. Mendoza," the teen interrupted him, "but hear me out."

"You'd better learn some respect, young man! I—"

Determined to be heard, Blake grabbed the older man's arm and held it tightly. He ignored the man's blustered cries to unhand him. Leaning in close, Blake hissed, "There's a bomb. Dynamite, at least. We've got to clear the school."

The principal jerked his arm free to stare at the teen. "How do you—"

"Just trust me," Blake begged. "Please."

Principal Mendoza sized up the young man, peering into his earnest but bruised face. His beseeching blue eyes looked vulnerable and scared. The principal couldn't miss the moisture pooling within their depths as the teen begged for his trust. Despite his current appearance and his highly unorthodox methods, Blake Reynolds was an ace student, a good athlete, and a well-behaved and popular student.

Mendoza made a snap decision. "You'd better to telling the truth," he murmured. Then he clapped Blake on the shoulder and gave a curt nod. His voice loud and booming, he spoke to the departing students, "Listen to your King! Hasten to the courtyard. Be quick, I say! Hurry along, ye royal subjects and ye peasants." He moved among them, sweeping his arms forward. "Single file, both doors, march along, march along. Your King has spoken!"

The auditorium was half empty when the first charge went off. Above the shriek of frightened students and the sudden thunder of their rushed footsteps, high-pitched alarms cut through the smoky air. Blake stayed behind with the teachers, making certain all students cleared the auditorium.

"You, too, Blake. Back door," Mr. Mendoza said sternly.

Blake shook his head. "I'll see this through."

"You've done your share, son." A smile touched the principal's face. "Go address your kingdom. Calm their fears. It's your duty as their king." He extended his palm to the teen, shaking Blake's hand with new respect. "You saved a lot of lives here today, Blake. You're a true hero."

"I don't know about that..."

"I do. Now go. Get out of here, so we can make sure everyone's out and safe."

Blake ran through the smoky hallway, seeing Bethani waiting for him on the other end.

As he stepped outside, sirens wailed. The army had arrived.


The fire department, Cutter included, made it in time to keep the fire to a minimum. Thanks to Blake's quick thinking, the dynamite did minimal damage to the building. It knocked bricks away and loosened some mortar, but no severe structural damage was done. Thanks to Bethani's sparkly pink belt and her expert knot tying, the ring leader of the gang was still bound to the railings when Brash arrived. His officers intercepted the three teens in the trees, and within the hour, Smokes was apprehended. All five teens were taken into custody and faced severe charges.

The auditorium would be closed until further notice, but other than minor smoke damage, the rest of the school was unharmed.

Still holding court outside, King Blake made a decree that school was canceled the following day. Principal Mendoza walked out in time to hear the cheering crowd and their chants of 'long live the king!'

"You forgot something inside, Mr. Reynolds," the principal said, holding up the plastic gold crown that was never awarded. "I believe this is yours, and justly so." As he placed the crown on Blake's blond head, the principal made a brief and flowery speech, thanking the teen for his quick thinking. He included Bethani and Mrs. Cooley in the accolades, giving credit where credit was due. He concluded by holding Blake's arm high into the air.

"Your king, Blake Reynolds, has spoken. No school tomorrow!"

If there ever was a doubt, Blake was now definitely a hero.

# 28

The wedding proceeded as planned. Given the day's events and Cutter's responsibilities with the fire department, Genny generously offered to postpone the ceremony until the next day, but her bridegroom wouldn't hear of it. He had waited long enough, he said, to make her his bride. After waiting for her his entire life, he wasn't putting off starting their life together for a moment longer.

At promptly seven o'clock, the church bells rang. Soft music filled the sanctuary. Bethani and Blake, bruises and all, lit the altar candles before taking their seats reserved for family. Like the rest of the wedding party, Bethani wore a red dress and Blake a red shirt.

With the lighting and atmosphere set, the ceremony began.

An audible gasp echoed throughout the church as Genny made her way down the rose-covered path. Her face aglow with happiness, she had never looked so beautiful. Her dimples appeared deeper than ever before, her eyes sparkled their most brilliant blue. Her dress was a creation of delicate white lace and tiny pink pearl beads. In typical Genesis style, it featured layers of frilly fullness, and a glimpse of her pink satin shoes.

But it was the look on Cutter's face—and the glimmer of tears in his eyes—that stole the breath from their guests. And when he surprised them all, including his bride, with a solo rendered in a surprisingly talented voice, there wasn't a dry eye in the house. Referencing the song they danced to one year ago on that magical night that led to the turning point in their relationship, Cutter sang his own version of 'The Lady in Red.' He changed the word red to *white*, lowered the higher notes to harmonize beautifully with the music, and left the room in hushed reverence when he finished.

And when the preacher pronounced them Mr. and Mrs. Cutter Montgomery, he let out an enthusiastic Aggie 'whoop!' and swept his new bride into his arms for an ecstatic kiss. As they made their way back down the aisle as husband and wife, Genny's tears freely flowed.

A wedding so memorable could only be followed with an equally grand reception. Plenty of rustic chic balanced the romantic red and pink theme into a look more stylish than cheesy. Good food, good friends, laughter, and high spirits flowed freely throughout the night.

By the time the couple fled to Cutter's truck—fully decorated with the customary streamers, shaving cream, cans, and cowbells, and with the special addition of his ever-present dog Diogee dressed as cupid—Madison's feet ached, and her head pounded. Even though it ended on a wonderfully happy note, the day had been long and grueling. Her children had been in danger. The fact weighed heavily on Maddy's mind, despite the jovial atmosphere around her.

"Just think," Brash said as he came from behind, wrapping his arms around her as the last of the guests finally left. "This will be us in five weeks and three days."

Madison released a dreamy sigh as she touched his cheek. She tipped her head back against his strong chest and closed her eyes. "I can hardly wait."

"We could cheat and find a justice of the peace to do the job sooner," he suggested as he tightened his hold around her waist.

"As tempting as that sounds, we can't do that to our families. I think they're as excited about our wedding as we are."

His words were a guttural rumble against her ear. "I doubt that." He pressed his body against hers as proof.

"Don't make those five weeks any harder than they already are," she begged. She couldn't resist reveling in the feel of him, imagining what would be.

"And three days." His tone was miserable.

Madison consulted her watch, a Valentine's Day gift from the man holding her. The custom sterling silver band featured hand-tooled hearts and their names intertwined among the scrolled designs. "Actually, it's more like two days and fourteen hours."

"Even without the five weeks, that's too long."

Madison echoed the sentiment as she hugged his arms to her. "I agree, my love."

Brash rested his chin on the top of her head. "Genny and Cutter had a great wedding, though."

"Who knew Cutter could sing like that!"

"Certainly not me."

"Everything was so beautiful. Genny was absolutely glowing."

"She's waited a long time to be a bride. I'm glad her day was perfect."

The worry crept back into Madison's voice. "It didn't begin that way. Brash, do you realize how close we came to a disaster today? We could have lost our children. All three of them."

"But we didn't, sweetheart. Once again, Blake saved the day. I am so stinking proud of that boy." The pride was evident in his rich voice. "He's become a real hero. And Bethani, too. They both averted a potentially deadly situation and saved an untold number of lives today."

"I can't even think about what could have happened. All those kids, trapped inside the auditorium…" She shuddered, just thinking about it. "What is wrong with people today? What kind of mind does it take to even *think* of setting fire to a school, or bombing it, or shooting it up? It's so sad that our world is reduced to this."

"All we can do is raise our children, the future generation, with the sense of right and wrong, and common decency. Teach them morals and the value of human life. And not to brag, but I think we've both done a jam-up job. Our three children are becoming very impressive young adults. It inspires hope, knowing such fine individuals are the leaders of tomorrow."

"If we can just keep them alive long enough to lead," Madison agreed in a melancholy voice. "Even if they survive—or prevent—school shootings and bombings, there's an even bigger risk of being hit by a drunk driver, or someone texting while driving. Both of which, by the way, are illegal but still happen every single day. Signing something into law doesn't always change things, especially the darkness in a person's soul."

Brash turned her around in his arms and declared, "Enough of this maudlin mood. Our children are safe, Genny and Cutter are happily married, and I need the warmth of a good-night kiss before I brave the cold and go home to my empty bed. Which," he added as solemnly as a vow, "I will magnanimously do for the next five weeks and two days, and not a single night after that, ever again."

"Never again." She breathed her own promise against his mouth.


Madison locked the door behind him, set the alarm, and wove her way through the downstairs rooms to turn off lights. They had done a brief sweep through the house earlier, picking up trash and blowing out candles. The rest could wait until morning.

She paused at the bottom of the stairs, smiling as she admired the leftover decorations and the lingering beauty of the evening. She was so happy for her friend, knowing Genny had found true love at last. The future was bright. For all of them.

Still smiling, Madison padded up the stairs, her long since abandoned heels dangling from her fingers. She turned to enter the upstairs library turned private office and came up short, seeing a woman standing in her private domain. The brief flare of panic gave way to a general sense of unease. She didn't remember seeing the woman among the reception guests, but there had been so many people swarming about the house. Perhaps she had simply missed her.

Still, something about the woman was vaguely familiar...

"I'm sorry," Madison said, trying not to sound as nervous as she felt. "I didn't realize we still had guests. I'm afraid the party is over."

The woman leveled her with a cold, impersonal gaze. "An excellent way of phrasing it." The words were spoken in heavily accented English, sending warning bells through Madison's already throbbing head.

The unfamiliar woman took a step forward. "Such an American saying, that." She reached into her belted coat, pulled a gun from the pocket, and aimed it directly at Madison. "The party eese, indeed, over."

"Who—Who are you, and what do you want?"

"It matters not who I am. It matters only if you choose to be smart and do as I say, or if you choose to be brave and to die. Do not move."

She couldn't if she wanted to. Madison's feet were glued to the floor.

"You have something that belongs to me. I want it back."

In all honesty, Madison replied, "I have no idea what you're talking about."

"There was something missing from the suitcase."

Things began to slowly click in Madison's mind. She thought she had seen this woman on the plane to Maryland, a couple of rows behind Beady Eyes. The woman with the impassive face. Did this make the woman a spy? Could this be the infamous and elusive Kalypso?

"Wait," she said, a sinking feeling invading her stomach. "Did my grandmother take the black light, after all?"

"Not the black light, you imbecile. The key!"

"Again, I have no idea what you're talking about." The woman wagged the gun. "Think."

"About what?" Madison cried. Despite the earlier warning, she turned to pace. "There wasn't a key. There were books and folders and pens. The black light," she added, trying to recall the exact contents, "and a ledger. Maybe a roll of mints."

"Think harder."

"Paper. Little blocks of paper, like sticky notes

without the sticky. That's it."

"Nothing you had to *snoop* for?"

Madison stopped pacing and frowned at the other woman. She hadn't been snooping! She went through the suitcase, hoping to find identification so she could return the suitcase to its rightful owner. "Of course not!"

The woman insisted otherwise. "My colleague saw you with the code," she accused.

Confused, Madison shook her head. "You said it was a key."

Her voice was impatient. "To a code."

Her head pounded, her feet hurt, her body ached with fatigue, and now her mind was muddled. Madison had endured enough.

"If you're talking about the note the little girl gave me at the airport, I turned it over to the CIA. You'll have to talk to them about it. Now if you'll kindly leave, I am exhausted, I have a headache, and I want to go to bed." She spoke bluntly, as if there weren't a gun pointed directly at her.

"I go nowhere without the key. It eese critical to the Lilac Code. I must have it back."

"I didn't take anything out!" Madison cried in exasperation. "I put every single thing back in the—" Even as she made the claim, a single slip of paper came to mind. She finished her emphatic claim, even if the last word lost some of its fire. "—suitcase."

She remembered the narrow ribbon of paper, tucked into the seams of the lining. It must have floated from the suitcase onto the floor, where she later stepped on it. That was the paper stuck to the bottom of her shoe when she first met Maury and Barton, aka Obukov and Murdoch, in the *Peralynna* game room.

Madison wouldn't have remembered that much, if

she hadn't run across that very note just yesterday, still stuffed in the pocket of her sweater. She remembered throwing the tiny scrap into the trashcan.

The woman saw the realization in Madison's eyes. "Where is it?" she demanded coldly.

"I—I threw it away."

"I do not believe you."

"Why would I keep it? There was nothing on it!"

"You lie."

"An inspector's code," Madison insisted.

"What was on the paper?" the woman demanded. She made a motion with her hand, reminding Madison she aimed a gun at her chest.

As if she could forget. Her only concern was keeping the woman away from the twins, sleeping peacefully in their beds.

"I will repeat myself but once," the woman ground out. "What was on the paper?"

It came to her in a rush, clearing her brain's fog like a brisk wind.

"Lilac!" Madison gasped.

It made sense now. The Lilac Code was a twist on the old Purple Cipher, with its sophisticated rotation of sixes and twenties. No wonder Marino thought she went to the *Cryptologic Museum* for insight into breaking the code. The strange books and endless lists within the suitcase were possible combinations, awaiting a key for deciphering. Old-school techniques for an old-school code. "The sixes," she breathed. More to herself than to the woman with the gun, she whispered, "There were six numbers. They were the master key."

Kalypso's voice was sharp. "What were the numbers?"

Startled back to reality, Madison blinked hard at

the other woman. "I—I have no idea."

"That eese most unfortunate for you." Kalypso cocked her pistol. "Without the paper, I have no reason to allow you to live."

An idea sprang to mind. "I threw it away. In that trashcan, behind the desk."

"Get it."

Madison stepped behind her desk, searching for something, *anything*, she could use as a weapon. There wasn't as much as a letter opener in sight.

"No funny beezness," the woman warned.

"Of course not." Madison dutifully picked up the ornate metal trashcan, testing its weight in her hands. It would have to suffice. She carried it with her as she approached the woman, pretending to dig in its depths for the paper.

"I think I feel it..." she said, running her hand inside.

Arming herself with the trashcan, wearing it on her hand like a boxing glove, Madison swung without warning. Her powerful blow took the other woman by surprise and knocked her to the ground. Madison fell on top of her, wrestling for control of the gun.

Their scuffle was short lived. Capitalizing on the element of surprise, Madison jerked the pistol from the other woman and whacked her across the head with it.

She didn't as much as blink. With a cold, menacing smile, Kalypso growled.

Madison knew a moment of pure fear. There was murder in the foreign woman's eyes.

In the blink of an eye, the agent's hands came up to grip Madison's neck and squeeze. Hard. Madison's breath came with a wheeze. Her eyes stung.

It took mere seconds. With oxygen denied, Madison felt herself growing weak.

"Drop your hands!"

She had never been so relieved to hear Brash's voice as she was in that moment. Yet, instead of lessening her hold, Kalypso's fingers tightened around her throat.

Brash repeated himself in a bark. "I said. Drop. Your. Hands."

The room grew fuzzy and dark. Madison, who sat astraddle the woman's waist, felt herself sag forward. She was vaguely aware of movement behind her. Probably the rogue agent's flailing legs as she put all her efforts into choking Madison to death.

Madison heard someone cry out in pain and wondered if it were her own voice. Yet how could she make a sound, when not as much as a breath escaped her throat? Was this truly the end?

She was lightheaded now. Even her throat felt lighter.

But the next sound, she knew, came from her. It was the hoarse, haggard rasp of a deep, greedy gulp of air.

Painful.

Exhilarating.

Life-saving.

Already on the verge of collapse, her lungs burned from the sudden influx of oxygen, but the knowledge registered on some level. She could breathe!

Madison fell away as the woman beneath her squirmed in pain. Brash's cowboy boot pinned her to the floor, unrelenting in its pressure. Madison may have even heard the snap of bone. Or perhaps it was the cocking of his gun, trained directly on the writhing woman.

He dared not look away. Eyes steady upon the intruder, he asked his fiancé, "You okay, sweetheart?"

Between coughs, she whispered, "Yes."

"Take my phone. Dial 911 and put me on speaker. I'm not taking any chances with this Jezebel."

With sluggish movement, Madison struggled to her feet and fished the phone from Brash's pocket. Her fingers were clumsy on the numbers. When dispatch answered, Brash gave detailed instructions on what to do, who to send, and where to come. By the time she disconnected, Madison's mind was clear enough to ask questions.

"How did you know to come back?"

"I always check the perimeter before I leave. I noticed the alarm was disabled."

Holding her throat, Madison spoke around the rawness. "But I set it." Even as she said it, she tried to remember hearing the beep of confirmation. Had she been too exhausted to miss such an important detail?

"Yeah, but it couldn't dial out. You didn't even know when I came in."

"True."

"I had to clear the downstairs before I made my way up here. I was almost too late." Though his eyes and his hold on the gun never wavered, his voice belied his weakness.

Hearing the break in his strong baritone, tears sprang to her eyes. "But you weren't. You saved me, Brash."

Now thick and rich, his voice wrapped around her with love.

"Five weeks and two days, Maddy," Brash assured her. "Nobody, especially some sniveling spy, is going to rob me of the day I make you my wife." He ground his foot in again for good measure, eliciting new cries of pain from the woman on the floor. "Find something we can tie her up with, sweetheart, until backup arrives."

"Bethani used a belt."

"Works for me. You can take mine off me, if you'd like."

The situation was dire. Kalypso, a notorious foreign spy for hire had walked into her home tonight in tiny little Juliet, Texas, penetrated the sanctuary of her bedroom suite, almost choked her to death to retrieve information vital to national security, and would have gladly orphaned Bethani and Blake (who had already faced one life-changing ordeal today) in the sake of greed. Greed, like Brash always said, was the root of all evil.

Despite all of that, Madison's eyes danced with a mischievous twinkle.

"Oh, I'd like," she assured him in a wicked, saucy drawl. "I can hardly wait to take that belt and that big ole' belt buckle off you. Unfortunately, now is not the time."

His words were but a growl. "Five weeks and two days, Maddy. Five weeks and two days."

A scratchy giggle escaped her raw throat. "They can't go by fast enough. After waiting for you half my life, I'll finally be Mrs. Brash deCordova."

Blake and Bethani Reynolds, along with Megan deCordova,
cordially invite you to attend the wedding of their parents
Madison Josephine Cessna Reynolds
and
Brash Andrew deCordova
in the next installment of The Sisters, Texas Mystery Series.

Watch for your invitation in the coming months.

# Note from Author

*The Columbia Inn at Peralynna* is quite real, and is used with the permission of its owners, David and Dr. Cynthia Lynn.

My husband and I first discovered this intriguing boutique bed and breakfast in September. We were charmed by the unique layout and, particularly, by our warm and gracious hosts. We returned in February, when the Lynns graciously showed us around their home and their community. (*Royal Taj Restaurant*, *The Iron Bridge Wine Company*, and the old Savage Mills cotton mill complex are also real places.) Cynthia and I spent many hours in the four story great room, discussing our mutual love for books and writing, and brainstorming future plots.

The inn has a fascinating story behind it. It is, indeed, fashioned after a CIA safe house in Germany that Cynthia thought of as her family's vacation home. She told me she simply thought their parents threw lots of parties and took their five children on spur-of-the-moment trips, often in the still of night. It was years before she realized her parents were spies and that those clandestine encounters were related to national security. In fact, the American pilot Francis Gary Powers (you probably remember the name from the blockbuster movie *Bridge of Spies*) was debriefed at the original safe house in Germany by her father.

During my last visit, I had the pleasure of listening to Cynthia and her sister recall memories of the house, their parents, and their unique lifestyle abroad. Oh, the books these women could write! The character of CIA Officer Logan McKee is, in fact, Cynthia's creation and will be the main character in a fiction series—non-classified, of course—that she plans to pen in the very near future. (No pressure, Cynthia. My readers are now salivating at the mouth, waiting to read the stories you've lived. If you don't come through, they're going to blame *me* for getting their hopes up. But like I said, no pressure, my friend.)

I hope you enjoyed this book and the glimpse shared into *The Columbia Inn at Peralynna*. The next time you're in the Baltimore/Columbia/DC area, you owe it to yourself to meet the Lynns and to stay in their beautiful home. Be sure and tell them I sent you. (And don't forget to look for those secret staircases!)

By the way, Boonsboro, Maryland is only an hour away, where you can visit *Turn the Page* bookstore and the *Boonsboro Inn*, both owned by author Nora Roberts.

Until next time,
Becki

# Crack the Lilac Code & Win!

Between now and July 17, 2018, you have the opportunity to WIN a free night stay in the penthouse suite at *The Columbia Inn at Peralynna*! Enter our Sweepstakes Contest at www.beckiwillis.com.

But never fear. If you don't capture the grand prize, you can still be a winner. Simply book your own visit to *Peralynna* at 410-715-4600, mention the secret code "Lilac" while doing so, and take 10% off your entire stay!

# ABOUT THE AUTHOR

Becki Willis, best known for her popular The Sisters, Texas Mystery Series and Forgotten Boxes, always dreamed of being an author. In November of '13, that dream became a reality. Since that time, she has published numerous books, won first place honors for Best Mystery Series, Best Suspense Fiction and Best Audio Book, and has introduced her imaginary friends to readers around the world.

An avid history buff, Becki likes to poke around in old places and learn about the past. Other addictions include reading, writing, junking, unraveling a good mystery, and coffee. She loves to travel, but believes coming home to her family and her Texas ranch is the best part of any trip. Becki is a member of the Association of Texas Authors, the National Association of Professional Women, and the Brazos Writers organization. She attended Texas A&M University and majored in Journalism.

You can connect with her at http://www.beckiwillis.com/ and http://www.facebook.com/beckiwillis.ccp?ref=hl. Better yet, email her at beckiwillis.ccp@gmail.com. She loves to hear from readers and encourages feedback!

# Books by Becki Willis

Forgotten Boxes
Tangible Spirits
He Kills Me, He Kills Me Not
The Mirror Series
    The Girl from Her Mirror
    Mirror, Mirror on Her Wall
    Light from Her Mirror
The Sisters, Texas Mystery Series
    Chicken Scratch – Book 1
    When the Stars Fall – Book 2
    Stipulations & Complications – Book 3
    Home Again: Starting Over – Book 4
    Genny's Ballad – Book 5
    Christmas In The Sisters – Book 6
    The Lilac Code, Book 7
Spirits of Texas Cozy Mystery Series
    Inn the Spirit of Legends – Book 1

# Sneak Peek:

# FORGOTTEN BOXES

*Named 2016 Best Suspense Fiction by Association of Texas Authors*
*Named 2017 Best Audio Book by Association of Texas Authors*

*Dedication and Special Thanks*
This book is dedicated to my parents, Billie and the late Benton Speer. Their love, support, and strong Christian guidance gave me the courage to believe in myself and follow my dreams.

I owe a special thank you to John Nugent for giving me a mini-lesson in the art and craft of maple syrup and sugaring. The story of ol' Merle and the evaporating sap was a true tale, compliments of Mr. Nugent. Names were changed to protect the innocent.

## CHAPTER ONE

The gate gave easily beneath her touch. A light brush of pressure was all it took for the old hinges to swing inward.

Any hint of resistance would have deterred her. That's all it would have taken for her to turn around, crawl back in her car, and leave behind this foolish notion of claiming her inheritance. Yet, the gate had opened with invitation, beckoning her inside the sleepy yard, and now Charity Gannon was halfway up the pebbled walk.

It all looked innocent enough. Idyllic, even. A tiny little cottage set in the middle of an over-sized lot, nestled beneath the arms of mature crabapple, cherry, and sugar maple trees. Window boxes and flowerbeds, an inviting screened-in summer porch. Peeling white paint for instant shabby chic charm. Signs of a vegetable garden off to the left, a weathered old shed to the right. A porch swing suspended from the limb of a huge old oak, surrounded by rose bushes and flowering shrubs.

Under normal circumstances, the charming scene would delight her. It looked like a clipping from one of those travel magazines, one that touted the hidden treasures of rural Vermont. The right travel agent could lease the cottage as the perfect summer retreat, garnering a hefty price tag for its quiet location and its nod to yesteryear.

Under normal circumstances, Charity might be tempted to rent the cottage herself. But there was nothing normal about her visit today, and she could not rent what she already owned.

In spite of the homey appearance of the cottage, a sense of dread spilled out onto the walkway and muddled around Charity's footsteps. Her pace slowed as she drew closer to the porch. Instead of cheerful window boxes, her eyes were drawn to the windows themselves, sad, empty panes that looked into a darkened house.

Charity tugged her sweater closer, gathering a handful of courage along with the fabric as she stepped onto the porch. The screen door protested with a loud screech, but it gave no more resistance than the foot gate out front. Maybe the front door would be less cooperative. Maybe the key would not fit. Maybe she could put this off until tomorrow.

But no, the old key was a perfect fit for the tarnished brass doorknob. The lock tumbled easily. As the door swung inward, Charity had no excuse not to step inside.

She stepped over the threshold and came to an abrupt halt. She was overwhelmed to see that the cottage was still fully furnished, filled with the remnants of someone else's life.

*Not just someone's*, she reminded herself. *Aunt Nell's*.

It was a small front room, crowded by too much furniture. There wasn't even enough room for a full-sized couch. An overstuffed loveseat snuggled next to an upholstered rocker. There was just enough room for a coffee table and a slender ladder back chair to complete the seating arrangement. Without the antique desk and overflowing bookcase, the room would have been cozy; with them, the space felt cramped.

Charity flipped a light switch, not expecting a reaction. She was surprised when golden light flooded from the glass globes of twin floor lamps.

She wandered into the adjacent dining room. Wide openings between the rooms gave the illusion of more space and offered a nice flow from one space to the next. The square oak table and china cabinet may or may not have qualified as antiques.

Like the living room, the space was crowded but neat. To the eye, there was nothing amiss; it was a small, modest home belonging to a widowed woman. Beneath the heavy cloak of stale air, Charity detected the clinging odors of onions, liniment, and old furniture polish.

But something else lingered in the air. Something not visible to the eye, something indiscernible by the nose. Whatever it was tickled the hairs on the back of Charity's neck and crawled down her spine with whispered unease.

"You're being silly." Charity spoke the words aloud, needing to hear a human voice in the eerie silence of the house. The rooms were mute, save for the steady click of time ticked away by the old-school clock in the living room. An occasional squeaky board protested beneath her feet, but not even the refrigerator hummed.

Charity stepped into the kitchen. It was large enough, but poorly designed. "How on earth did she ever cook an entire meal in here?" She propped indignant hands upon her hips as she gave a pitied 'tsk'. Her eyes roamed over the sad lack of laminate-topped counter space, ancient appliances, and a stove that stood all the way across the room, separate from other features of the kitchen.

"That door must go outside, and I guess this one," she murmured as she stepped through the doorway on her left, "takes me to... a teeny, tiny hall. Okay, so there's the bathroom. Love the old claw-foot tub, not so much the tiny mirror and medicine cabinet... Down the four-foot hall into… a shoebox. A shoebox with a bed and an old wardrobe. So no closet. Unless this door… nope, goes to the other bedroom." As she left the tiny room she muttered, "A pass-through shoe-box, at that."

She continued her monologue as she entered the

front bedroom. "Old style house, no closets, no hall to speak of, just rooms opening into other rooms. Since this door opens back into the living room, it is one big loop. Tour is over, ladies and gentleman," she murmured.

With puffed out cheeks, Charity turned back to survey the largest of the bedrooms; 'largest', however, being a relative term.

"So this was obviously the master." Again, a large antique wardrobe served as a closet. A dresser and nightstands on either side of the quilt-covered bed provided more storage. A full bed, she noted, not even a queen, but plenty big for one person. That left hardly enough space to squeeze around the bed and reach the window, where a puffy cushion turned a long cedar chest into a window seat.

A collection of men's toiletries littered the bedside table farthest from the door. A man's suit of clothing hung from the hall tree tucked in a corner.

"Auntie Nell, did you have a lover?" She spoke to an empty room, but her voice held a teasing lilt. The rest of the house had a decided feminine touch — plenty of frilly pale yellow throw pillows, rose-speckled chintz on the loveseat, frou-frou and lace doilies scattered here and there — but here in the bedroom there were definite traces of a man.

Charity took a step closer to examine the outfit. The tattered khaki work clothes appeared to be from a different era.

"How sad," she murmured. "All these years, she kept her husband's clothes." The knowledge added to the heaviness in the stale air.

Charity knew very little about her uncle. His name

was spoken in hushed tones; not the kind reserved for the well-loved, highly revered heroes who still inspired awe and respect, but the kind that were whispered in shame, or pity, or some sad mixture of the two. Charity wasn't even born when Harold Tillman died. No one shared the details of his death with her, no one ever bothered to tell her the story. All she knew was that his death pushed her aunt ever closer to the edge of sanity, and further away from the comfort and support of her only sister. By the time Charity's own mother died, the women barely spoke to one another. Aunt Nell came for Laura's funeral but Charity remembered how she kept to herself, curled into a ball of self-pity and grief. She left immediately after the service.

In the sixteen years that passed since her mother's death, Charity heard from her aunt exactly twice. The lack of response never kept Charity from sending Christmas cards and graduation announcements to her sole relative on her mother's side, but the only time Nell ever replied was when she sent a crisp one hundred dollar bill for Charity's eighteenth birthday, along with the scrawled words, '*Your mother would have been so proud of you.*' The next and only other time Charity heard from her aunt was when the lawyer called, saying Nell had passed away and left her estate to her sole niece.

So here she was, come to collect a reward she hardly deserved.

*Why me?*

Charity asked the question a hundred times, but there was no clear answer. Even if she was Nell's only blood kin, surely there had been others more deserving of the honor. Charity barely remembered her aunt; had, in fact, seen her but a handful of times in her life. Surely, there were friends or neighbors who deserved to be rewarded for the part they played in Nell Tillman's life. Someone who knew the real story behind her uncle's death and why his name was spoken with pity, someone who knew why these walls fairly crumbled with the weight of a heavy conscience.

There was so much more to the story, Charity was certain of it. She could feel the oppression in the air. It wasn't just the musty smell of dust and the lack of fresh air. There was a story to be told in the strictly feminine decor, save for the untouched male garments here in the bedroom. Something happened to her uncle, Charity was sure. Something bad, something of which no one spoke.

Charity fingered the ragged garments. They must have been hanging there for at least twenty-five years or more. A thick layer of dust coated the material. At her touch, the disturbed motes danced up to tickle her nose and caused Charity to sneeze. She inadvertently jerked, disturbing the clothes even further. A fold shifted to reveal a dark stain across the front of the shirt. Even after all these years, the blood was evident.

Just like the bullet hole it surrounded.

Charity dropped the cloth with a jerk, her hand stinging. Her sudden move caused the hall tree to teeter uncertainly, twirling on one foot as if the wooden pole had a life of its own. The bloodstained clothes whipped around and chased after Charity as she shrieked and stumbled backwards.

After a balancing act worthy of a circus performance, the pole finally righted itself and spun to a stop. The blood soaked clothes made a final swish through the air, circled round the pole, then settled once more into a sagging heap.

"Oh. My. Gosh." Charity whispered the words aloud, palms flat against her cheeks. She stood staring at the clothes, wondering if they would take another lunge at her. With much of the dust shaken free and now floating through the air, tickling at her nose once more, the clothes looked lighter, freer. Their secret was no longer hidden in the folds of forgotten khaki. The bloodstains — and the bullet hole — were now clearly visible.

Charity knew it was irrational, but she glanced over her shoulder with a sense of guilt. The rush of relief washing over her was every bit as crazy. She couldn't say exactly why, but she hurried forward and rearranged the clothes so that their secret was once again safe. Then she quickly left the room, even shutting the door behind her for good measure.

Out of sight and, she hoped, out of mind.

# Sneak Peek:

# TANGIBLE SPIRITS

*Finalist for Upcoming 2018 Reward of Novel Exellence (RONE) Paranormal Long Fiction by InD'Tale Magazine Named 2018 Best Paranormal Fiction by Association of Texas Authors*

*Special Note from the Author*

The following story is set in the very real town of Jerome, Arizona and, to the best of my knowledge, the historical anecdotes are true. However, I've taken the liberty of blending bits of truth, bits of fancy, to craft this story. While the landmarks—including the *Sliding Jail*, *Cuban Queen Bordello*, and the old *Bartlett Hotel*—are real, all businesses and characters exist only in my imagination. The blasts, Spanish Expeditions, and Executive Order 6102 are all a matter of record.

My husband and I first visited Jerome in May, where the unique architecture of the town and the ghost legends immediately intrigued me. In September, my daughter and I returned to do in-depth research. We stayed in a "haunted" hotel, engaged in ghost tours, and soaked up as much lore, legend, and history as possible. Thank you, Winter, for helping me research and for making it a fun and productive mother/daughter trip!

I also want to thank Jane Goddard for her invaluable information, dienel96 for a wonderful cover, and *you* for reading.

# CHAPTER ONE

*Dead* was dead. Gera didn't believe in ghosts.

That was why this assignment rankled her so. Why was she, of all people, assigned to a story about ghosts? The magazine might as well have sent her to the North Pole to interview Santa Claus himself.

It was bad enough being surrounded by desert. Miles and miles of barren terrain, the flat Arizona landscape broken only by scattered saguaro cacti and shrubs. No real trees to speak of. Plenty of bushy, thorny shrubs and desert plants. The most interesting thing she had seen so far was the odd warning sign for a wild donkey crossing.

With rays of heat beaming down from the cloudless azure sky, today promised to be a scorcher, but she could handle the heat. The dry, blustery wind was a nuisance, sweeping across her skin like sandpaper and playing havoc with her hair. Why had she even bothered with a comb this morning? She could simply add gel to the spikes and go for that edgy, badass look so many reporters favored.

Lord knew she needed all the edge she could get.

The further north she traveled, away from the armed cacti that stood like sentries along the roadside, the elevation climbed. The famed saguaros of the Sonora desert gave way to a multitude of prickly pear, intermingled with bushy shrubs and a few more trees. The Black Hills of Yavapai County rose in the distance, teasing the eye with variety, beckoning travelers onward.

Pulling Gera closer to her assignment.

"There are ghosts in them thar hills," she drawled aloud. Her voice dripped with sarcasm.

"Your first big story with the rag, and it may be your last." Gera gave voice to the pessimistic thought as she sped down the highway, racing toward the faraway mountains. She grumbled to an empty audience in her rented sedan, giving free reign to her frustrations. "I don't know what Jillian was thinking, sending me in for this one. I wanted to cover the story on the new cancer hospital opening in Dallas. Seniority shouldn't be the only deciding factor on who gets what story, should it? Enthusiasm should count for something. *Believability* should count for something! How am I supposed to give a fair and unbiased report on something I don't even believe exists?"

Some people, such as her Aunt Geraldine, believed that lives were recycled. How else, her aunt insisted, did one explain déjà vu, that sense of walking into a building one had never been in before, and knowing its exact layout and feel, right down to the rear exit? The obvious answer, according to her aunt, was that one had been there before, in another life.

And how, her namesake wanted to know, did she explain love at first sight, if not for the fact that souls were already acquainted from another time, another life? How did she explain pets that were as smart as human beings, if not for reincarnation? Life was simply too precious to discard with the cessation of breath. Aunt Geraldine believed that when one host body died, the soul found another body in which to reside.

Other people, such as her grandmother, believed that upon death, souls were sent either to Heaven or to Hell, depending on one's time here on Earth. The good, pious souls were granted eternal life. The disobedient were banished to the devil.

Gera liked the thought of eternal life, but she still had her doubts. Grams dragged her along to Sunday school when she was a little girl. Taught her about the

Bible and the perils of good and evil. Yet her grandmother was also the one to tell her about the Easter Bunny and the magical Tooth Fairy, not to mention a jolly old elf that drove a team of miniature reindeer upon people's rooftops. Grams—who never lied—had a theory about how one man could deliver presents to good little boys and girls around the world at seemingly the same time. Something about wind currents and the flux in temperatures worldwide, compounded by time zones and language barriers. The strange phenomenon caused some clocks to stall inexplicably, while others raced forward, bringing time to a virtual standstill for the course of one evening. Much to young Gera's dismay, none of those fanciful notions panned out. Would the concept of Heaven be any different?

Still others believed in a third option. Some—though certainly not Gera Stapleton—believed that a person's spirit could linger on Earth before crossing over to the other side. Something to do with unfinished business in life.

But did anyone ever have their lives pulled together and neatly tied with a bow? Didn't everyone leave behind unfinished business? While Gera liked the thought of one last opportunity to right the wrongs she had done in life, even from the grave, the idea sounded no more plausible than streets paved in gold.

Her co-worker Ramon was one such believer. During a séance last fall, the seasoned reporter insisted he had spoken with a beloved relative who was taken from life too soon. Ramon volunteered as a ghost-walk tour guide in downtown Notre Dame. He refused to accept money for his time, saying it was an honor to walk among the spirits and share their stories. Her co-worker was sincere in his belief, as certain about ghostly spirits as Grams was about the Holy Spirit and Aunt Geraldine was about reincarnation.

In Gera's mind, *dead* was just that—dead. No afterlife, no recycled spirits, no caught between worlds. Just dead.

She stewed for a while, railing against the injustice of it all. Ramon was the obvious choice for this story. His '08 Corolla had bumper stickers that said, 'I see dead people' and 'I'd rather be ghost hunting.' He watched the full array of television programs devoted to spirit sightings and haunted places. Ramon would've done this story better justice than she could. Even Gera knew that.

Ghost stories were all the rage these days. A few years ago, just the rumor of being haunted was a stigma hotels could little afford. These days, an in-house ghost meant instant fame and fortune.

The town of Jerome, Arizona was a perfect example. According to locals, ghosts freely roamed through the small town of less than five hundred people. Instead of scaring visitors away, tourists flocked to the mountainside community, hoping to see the visions for themselves. Television shows and ghost hunters alike joined the melee, eager to capture the spirits on film or meter. Not so long ago, the historic mining town was destined for extinction. Now it enjoyed new life through old spirits, and gave fresh meaning to the term 'Arizona ghost town.'

The town even had its very own resident ghost, a friendly apparition named Mac. Residents spoke of him as if he were an old friend. However, a recent string of mischief and petty crimes had taken place in the small town, and rumor had it that Mac was to blame. *When It Happens Magazine* thought it was worth investigating, so they sent in their newest reporter, Gera Stapleton. They even booked her in one of the town's more notoriously known haunted hotels.

"I just hope the ghosts don't rattle their chains and moan all night long. I need all the beauty rest I can get." She glanced into the visor mirror. "Especially with this hair."

Half an hour later, Gera turned off the interstate. The terrain here was higher and dotted with green. Not nearly as high as the San Francisco Peaks in the distance, but at least the dirt swelled with hills and valleys, many of them congested with actual green, leafy trees.

Until now, Gera hadn't realized how fond she was of the willowy giants. Trees reminded her of a simpler, gentler time, when she and her cousins climbed in the trees at their grandmother's farm. They would hang upside down from the sturdy limbs, studying the clouds as they rolled across the sky on a lazy summer afternoon. Robbed a snack from crab apple and pear trees heavy with fruit. Built a fort in a favorite old oak, where they spent long hours slaying dragons and fighting off pirates, hiding from Indian attacks and enemy soldiers. And on rare occasions, when her male cousins agreed, they played house, where she stirred up dishes of mud, leaves, and pecans, and served them in salvaged bits of pottery and metal scavenged from the burn pile.

A smile lingered on Gera's face as she recalled the fun they had over those long summer visits. The farm was gone now, sold to a developer who turned the orchards into a strip mall and the goat meadow into an apartment building. One of those upscale ones, with a coffee shop and deli on the ground floor, and boutiques that sold trendy clothing, scented soaps, and fake tans. Progress, they called it.

The further north Gera traveled, the more

impressed she became.

"Oh, wow. Now this is gorgeous!" Gera wiggled excitedly in her seat, thrilled to see the impressive red rock formations looming ahead. She thought of all those old westerns her father liked to watch on Saturday afternoons, the ones with bigger-than-life heroes cast against backdrops just like these.

After stopping for a bite to eat in the picturesque town of Sedona, she hit the road with more enthusiasm. Iconic formations gave way to clustered canyons and foothills. As the elevation rose, so did her spirits. She passed through an idyllic canyon canopied by trees. Drove alongside a gurgling river stream. Gazed up at impressive rocky ledges on either side of the road. Hugged mountain curves and prayed no one crossed the yellow line that separated her lane from the oncoming traffic.

She hoped to reach Jerome before dusk. She needed daylight as she traversed the squiggled blacktop road weaving its way up Mingus Mountain. A series of switchbacks and sharp curves sharpened her awareness and set her nerves on edge. Going up wasn't so bad. It was coming down that already worried her.

Signs along the roadway tracked her progress. Two more miles to Jerome. Another sharp curve, another incline. Another sign, this one announcing the altitude of five thousand feet. A few more twists, and she had just one mile to go.

The first glimpse of the town came into view. A few rooftops jutted through the trees, perched along a ledge on the side of Cleopatra Hill. The structures at the top of the mountain's peak beckoned her, but after a half dozen switchbacks and yet another mile, she still hadn't reached them. She passed a sign welcoming her to Jerome, Arizona, Elevation 5246,

Founded 1876.

More buildings came into view, stacked one upon the other in layers against the mountain. Gera stared in amazement at the many tiers of the town. She had read somewhere that the town was propped against a thirty-degree slope, two thousand feet above the Verde Valley floor. Until now, she hadn't realized how precarious thirty degrees would look. There had to be at least fifteen hundred vertical feet between the top and bottom tiers of the town.

"This could be interesting, in a slide-off-the-mountain kind of way," she decided aloud. She peered through the windshield, trying to get a better look at the mountaintop ahead. "Maybe this gig won't be so bad, after all."

She made another curve and followed the one-way street up yet another hill. Hull Street led past a tiny string of old buildings, through parking spaces on either side of the street, past an oddly leaning stone structure, and to another small collection of buildings at the top of the hill. The town's main street was one block over.

The one marked with all the crime scene tape and the coroner's van.

## CHAPTER TWO

Emergency vehicles lined the streets, their red and blue strobe lights casting an unnatural glow into the fading light of day. It had taken longer to wind up the mountain than she anticipated.

The journalist inside her demanded that she stop, even before she saw the police officer. He waved her down, stepping up to the side of her vehicle with his yellow flashing wand.

"Sorry, but I need to ask you to wait for a few minutes while crews work the scene."

"What happened, Officer?"

"Tending to a bit of business, Miss," he said evasively.

Working a hunch, Gera flashed her press badge. "I'm with the press."

The officer looked surprised. "How did you guys already get wind of this? We just found the body, not twenty minutes ago." He waved his wand to the car behind her, halting their progress. "Only reason the coroner is here is 'cause he was already on the mountain. This is Tuesday night poker with the boys."

He didn't question which media she was affiliated with, so Gera took it as a sign. Here was her chance to work a real story, not some fluff piece about a ghost. "Where do I park?" she asked quickly, taking advantage of the moment.

"Uh, just pull down there in the parking lot and walk up the hill," he decided. "Show them your badge and tell them Royce cleared you."

"Thanks, Royce!"

Gera whipped the car into the empty parking area to her left. Grabbing her camera and her recorder, she looped her badge lanyard over her head as she made her way up the hillside. Emergency vehicles blocked off the street directly in front of her, leaving her pathway clear.

The building facing her was but a skeleton. At least two stories of brick, stone, and metal railings. Intriguing arches and empty chambers. Gera could only see the side profile of the gutted structure. The front of the building faced Main Street, parallel to the one she arrived upon. A growing crowd assembled there, cast in the strobing shadows of blue and red.

A uniformed man stepped from the gathering shadows and blocked her progress. "Sorry, Miss, this entire block is quarantined."

"It's okay, I'm with the press." She flashed her badge with breezy confidence. "Royce already cleared me." She turned and waved down the hill, pretending the other man could see.

The officer squinted his eyes, studying her as if he noticed vines sprouting from her ears. "Who called you?" he demanded. "I've never seen you before."

Gera countered with, "Does it really matter?" She looked beyond him, to the stretcher lifted from the lower levels of the ruins. "What happened?"

The officer turned to watch the progress of his fellow first responders. "Looks like Abe Cunningham fell to his death."

Gera eyed the ornate iron railings across the front of the missing wall, thinking they were reminiscent of a jail cell. Too tall to go over, too narrow to slip between, the bars created an effective barrier between the sidewalk and the exposed stone floor below. She edged closer, trying to judge the distance of the fall. From the sidewalk, it would be an easy fifteen feet. Her eyes scanned the brick walls on two sides of the skeletal structure, imagining how a person might scale the excessive height in order to plummet to their death. The buildings were from another era, when twelve and fifteen-foot ceilings were standard. At one time, this had been a two-story building with a sub-level, even though the sky was now its only ceiling.

"How did he get through?" She had the recorder whirring, awaiting his reply.

"Best as we can tell, Mac pushed him."

Gera tried, but she couldn't temper the astonishment that bled into her voice. "Mac? You're blaming a ghost for this death?"

The officer pushed the hat up from his forehead and scratched at the crease it left behind. "Folks reported seeing ole Mac right here on the corner, minutes before Abe came along. No one else was on the sidewalk. Seems to be the only explanation so far."

"Assuming I believed the ghost was responsible— and that is a huge assumption, by the way—how do you explain Abe getting from this sidewalk to that lower level?" Gera gestured with her hands to mark each spot. "Even if this 'ghost' could slip between the bars, how do you explain a full-grown man getting past them?"

She raised a valid argument, but the officer wasn't impressed. Instead, he looked her over again. His gaze was skeptical. "Who did you say you were?"

She thrust out her hand for a firm handshake. "Gera Stapleton, *When It Happens Magazine*. And you are?"

"Officer Mike Cooper."

"So, Officer Cooper, who discovered Mr. Cunningham's body?"

"That would be Grant Young," he said. He nodded to the man speaking to another officer in low, confidential tones. "He noticed Abe lying on the floor below and immediately called for help, but it was too late. Abe was already gone."

"Do you have any idea how long he had been down there?"

"Witnesses saw him pass along the street less than an hour ago, so not long."

"And you don't think it was a suicide?"

The policeman gave her a sharp look. "Why would Abe want to kill himself?"

"I have no idea. You tell me."

"Now, look. If you're talking about that misunderstanding with the bank, he got all that cleared up…"

Using an old reporter trick, Gera looked non-convinced, even as she shrugged. "If you say so."

On the defensive for his late friend, the officer unwittingly stepped into her trap. "What? You think there really was something to him owing all that money in back taxes?"

"I never said that."

"But you insinuated it," he accused. His lips curled in derision. "All you reporters are the same. You get one whiff of controversy, and you blow it all out of proportion. So Abe got a little behind in his taxes. So what? He paid them in full before the state started proceedings. There's no way he would've offed himself over that, so don't even go there."

Somewhat amused at the officer's angry retort to her fishing expedition, Gera made nice and backed off. "You know what? I think you're right. But tell me. Why would your friendly ghost Mac want to kill Abe?"

"Because lately, Mac hasn't been so friendly."

"Why do you think that is?" She cocked her head to one side, pretending not to be asking about the personality quirks of a ghost, of all things. Had her journalism degree come down to this?

She worked long and hard to get that degree. She started college later in life than most of her classmates, at least six years older than the incoming freshman class. Even after working two jobs all that time to pay tuition, she only had enough saved up for one year. During her eighteen-month hiatus from school, she worked four part-time jobs. There had been times when she met herself coming and going, juggling the different schedules as she worked herself to a frazzle and enrolled in online classes. The grueling pace almost landed her in the hospital. When she scored a position at the newspaper, doing grunge work for the assistant editor's assistant, she allowed herself the luxury of quitting one of her jobs. Her stint as a night janitor was the first to go, even though it paid slightly more than her gig at Crispy Chicken Delight. If she ever saw a mop bucket or a deep fryer again in this lifetime, it would be too soon for her. It took her longer than expected, but last year, at the ripe old age of thirty-one, Gera trotted across the stage and accepted her diploma.

It was the single greatest accomplishment in her life.

And here she squandered that degree, inquiring about a ghost who supposedly killed a man.

Officer Cooper never knew how difficult it was for Gera to ask that question, how hard it was for her to keep the look of interest upon her face. He thought it perfectly normal to discuss a ghost.

He actually looked worried. "We haven't figured that out yet. For almost eighty years, ole Mac has been roaming this town, friendly as can be. Been known to help out more than a few times, stepping in to guide someone out of the way of traffic, finding lost items, keeping watch over the town when times were hard. One time, back when I was just a kid, little Dewey Miles fell down in one of the old mine shafts. Mac was the one to lead searchers right to the boy. So, you can see why we're all stumped, wondering what the heck has gotten into him after all this time. I hate to say it, but Mac has been downright ornery these past few months." He looked over his shoulder, to the closing doors on the coroner's vehicle. "And now this."

No, Gera didn't see. She didn't see how an entire town could be so naive. An abandoned mineshaft was the obvious place to look for a missing child. Lost items turned up every day, even without the benefit of a ghost. Why did they credit a dead man for these everyday deeds? And why did they blame him now for a death?

Jillian briefed her on the town's history—brief being the operative word—before Gera boarded the plane, but the details were still sparse. Perhaps Officer Cooper could fill in some of the gaps.

"So, Mac has been roaming these streets for almost eighty years, huh?" She tried her best to sound conversational. In her wildest imaginations, this was never a conversation she saw herself in.

The policeman nodded. "That's right. Jerome was a big mining town, back in the day. Pulled over thirty-three million tons of copper, gold, silver, and more from the depths of these mountains; over a billion dollars' worth, even way back then. Old Horace McGruder—Mac to his friends—was killed in a blasting accident back in '38, the same one that sent our jail over there sliding down the hill." He nodded toward the oddly slanted structure Gera noticed on the way into town. "He's been seen roaming around town ever since. When they pulled his body from the blast site, he was missing an ear. Some folks say he's been searching for it all these years, not willing to cross over until he was a whole man again."

Not just a ghost, but a one-eared ghost. Now that was a new one.

"Hey, Mike!"

The officer turned to see who called his name. Gera knew her time was slipping away.

"Just one more thing before you go," she pressed. "Does Abe Cunningham have a family?"

His face was suitably mournful. "He did," he said, sadly emphasizing the past tense. "He and Ruth have been married forever. They must have at least a dozen grandchildren. This will hit them hard."

"Where did Mr. Cunningham live?"

Irritation crossed the policeman's face. "Now look, don't you go snooping around Ruth, stirring up troubles where none exist."

Gera shook her head in denial. "For identification purposes," she was quick to assure him.

An odd look replaced the irritation. His nose flared, as if he had gotten wind of a foul smell. "Do you feel that?" His voice was lower than before.

A slight breeze stirred the evening air. After the heat of the day, it was a welcomed respite. "The breeze? Yes, it's nice."

He shook his head. "Not the breeze. The chill. One of them is here."

Gera looked around. "One of whom? One of Abe's family?"

"No. One of the ghosts."

CPSIA information can be obtained
at www.ICGtesting.com
Printed in the USA
LVHW05081907O719
623350LV00012B/375